When n
Bloom

More Tales From The Forest

Mark Billen

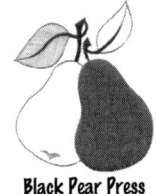

Black Pear Press

When The Gorse Is In Bloom

First published in April 2017 by Black Pear Press
www.blackpear.net

ISBN 978-1-910322-34-5

Cover design by Black Pear Press

Dedication

For everyone who has enjoyed the richness of rural life.

Readers' reviews of **Tales From The Forest** (which is also published by Black Pear Press - www.blackpear.net) by purchasers on Amazon:

A wonderful, humorous book full of fascinating characters and many chickens! This is an England as many of us remember, but which is sadly all but disappearing, except in The Forest.

This is a very recently published book, but I am sure that, like me, people will be champing at the bit for more once they have read this one. So please, Mark, let's have another or two! Can't wait!

***

If you would like a picture painted of life in country England in the post war years, told thru a montage of short stories, this is the book for you.

Each story is told in a charming, often amusing, but easy style, based close to the truth, but all centred round a fictitious village in middle England. The more stories I read, the more I enjoyed the book. As a senior citizen, I could relate to each tale. Please write more, Mark.

Acknowledgements

I must give thanks to all who have encouraged me to publish these stories. So often, when a tale is told one hears, 'You really ought to write that down.' That is what I have done. I would also like to acknowledge the support I have received from many people and especially Black Pear Press.

Mark Billen's *'Tales From The Forest'* and *'When The Gorse Is In Bloom…'* contain stories developed from reminiscences of life in southern England.

Mark also writes plays for schools and drama groups. They have been performed in the United Kingdom and also in USA, Canada and Australia as well as in international schools in Ethiopia, Singapore, Sri Lanka, Switzerland, France and China.

A recent youth theatre play by Mark is *'Cinderella's Sisters – Happy Ever After?'* continuing the story of Clorinda and Tisbe after the wedding of their sister. The first production was given by Dreamaker Drama Academy, Beijing. Latest youth theatre plays by Mark are *'Beastly Baron Counterblast'* and *'All Right! Snow White!'*

In 2015 Mark completed *'The Red King',* a satirical farce set in the future. This is Mark's first play intended for adults to perform.

Mark has also written a series of children's books for young readers featuring *Henry Bear And His Cousin Fred* together with their friends. These books are published in aid of the charity Action for Children.

Plays By Mark Billen

The Love For Three Oranges
The Zoron
www.schoolplayproductions.co.uk

Bl…Bl…Bluebeard!
All In The Stars…
Perfect Pupil
Seeking Sleeping Beauty
Cinderella's Sisters…Happy Ever After?
www.lazybeescripts.co.uk

Aladdin's Arabian Nightmare
The Red King
www.comedyplays.co.uk

Beastly Baron Counterblast
All Right! Snow White!
www.schoolplayscripts.co.uk

Children's Books

Henry Bear And His Cousin Fred Series
The Crunching In The Night
www.henryandfred.co.uk

Foreword

It has been a delight to remember rural life of southern England when writing this collection of stories. The Forest, the market town of Humbury, the villages Whytteford, Chamford, Breamhill, and the cathedral city of Salchester are all representative of English life from the not-so-distant past. The characters, likewise, do not exist except in my mind but as each tale is told you may become fond of some of them and infuriated by others. There are stories full of humour but also accounts of sad events. Surely that is how we travel through life?

Contents

When The Gorse Is In Bloom…

'I sees the garse is in bloom,' murmured my grandfather as I helped him one balmy day. I was sixteen and had discovered the delights of young ladies of my own age. My first girlfriend was Amy, a petite beauty with long blond hair and an enchanting smile that lured me to her.

'But the gorse is always in bloom,' I replied. Gorse blooms freely in the autumn and winter but normally, whatever the season, there are some flowers on any gorse bush.

'That's roight, the garse never stops flarring.' There was a chuckle after he spoke; my grandfather was teasing me but I wasn't quite sure what he was hinting at. 'An' we knows what folks say abart the garse being in bloom. Don' we?'

'What's that? I asked.

'Why,' said Grandpa, 'what folks say is…' Here he seemed to pause for effect. 'What folks say is…when garse is in bloom then loving's in fashion.' And he gave another chuckle.

When the gorse is in bloom loving's in fashion…

Throughout The Forest gorse bushes are scattered on scrubland where little else grows. The soft young gorse tips are eaten by the hard-tongued donkeys that happily munch on most things they can find. The bright yellow flowers of the bushes add a splash of colour in the most sombre days of the year. In hot weather fires sometimes sweep across the open land. The gorse burns fast as the flames tear through it leaving earth and sticks well blackened. After a scrubland fire soft green growths of gorse begin to appear and within a few weeks the bushes recover their strength.

It was quite clear that my grandfather had heard some gossip that had spread from Whytteford to Chamford and he was enjoying teasing me. I really didn't mind.

'Don't worry,' he said, smiling gently, 'your secret's safe with me.'

If it had still been a secret then Grandpa would have kept quiet enough; instead he was enjoying himself. 'An' another thing,' he added. 'When there's no garse blooms, why, then…kissing's out of fashion!'

My family lived at Whytteford, a village on the edge of The Forest that has existed for many centuries. A little Saxon church sits in a quiet valley; cottages made from wattle and daub still survive. Woodland areas are nearby but so are farms and open common land where animals roam and the heather blooms in the summer. On the common you can see signs of historic occupation and hints of crude cultivation. Here and there is an ancient tumulus; an earth lump on the landscape with a useful hollow in the centre, popular with young lovers but usually frequented by rabbits. The centre of the village is near the Cobblers Arms, a traditional public house where local ale is poured down parched throats and gossip is gathered. Any news from Whytteford soon spread to other villages.

Nearby is Chamford; a historic village with an ancient

hostelry, The Brown Bear, which is reputed to be haunted. Down a narrow leafy lane lived my grandparents. My grandfather enjoyed working in the garden of their cottage and he also kept some chicken that he almost revered. My grandmother often thought that Grandpa gave his hens more attention than he gave her. I enjoyed visiting their quaint cottage and often worked with Grandpa in his tidy garden.

The flowing summer was full of hot days and warm still evenings and Grandpa kept referring to gorse. Here and there patches of yellow gorse bloomed throughout The Forest and another girl was attracting my attention. This was Louisa, a tall dark-haired beauty who was full of humour and physical delights that more than charmed me.

As we gathered broad beans from his garden my grandfather's twinkling eyes looked across at me. 'The garse is very…er…flowery this year, I'm told.'

'What do you mean?'

'Ohhhhhhhhh,' he drawled, 'I keep my ears open and my eyes too. It's surprising whart one 'ears and what'n sees.'

'The beans are big,' I said trying to divert the conversation. Grandpa always grew his beans and peas until they were very fulsome. The trouble with them was that they were always so big and hard that eating them was best avoided as no amount of chewing softened them.

'T'would be a good idea to walk a bit further from lanes and go deeper into the woods.' He spoke kindly. 'You'll only be young once so make the most of it,' he added almost conspiratorially. 'Take some walks. Mabel always used to say Woodbine Wood was very comfortable. When the woodbine is warmed by the evening sun the scent from the flowers is very sweet. In fact,' he added his eyes staring straight at me, 'it might be said that scent of the woodbine is quite seductive.'

Great Aunt Mabel had been quite wistful when she told me about Woodbine Wood and my grandfather seemed to be confirming its reputation.

In autumn The Forest colours were at their richest but gradually the trees were stripped of their leaves. Fungi were in abundance, nuts, acorns and chestnuts fell.

The snow came in the New Year and the gorse provided colour poking out from beneath white decorations that nature had provided. Winter walks in The Forest had to be taken with care as the ground might be frozen hard one day, softening the next day and treacherous in no time at all.

'Is the garse still bloomin'?' asked my grandfather one cold January day.

'Very nicely,' I replied. We seemed to have developed a coded conversation. Grandpa liked to know what was happening in my life. Although he was well past seventy he still liked to 'admire the scenery' and was gently inquisitive about my love life.

Eventually it was time for me to return home. The sun was setting, the sky cold and the air bitter. Grandpa saw me to the cottage gate.

'You need something to cuddle to keep you'm warm on an evenin' like this,' he said as I was leaving. 'It's good to keep the fires burning brightly.' Chuckling to himself he clicked the gate shut then turned away to walk to the bottom of his garden and shut up the chicken before the foxes began to roam.

Suddenly he turned and called out to me, 'It's noice when the garse is in bloom! The more it blooms the better! Keep the garse blooming!'

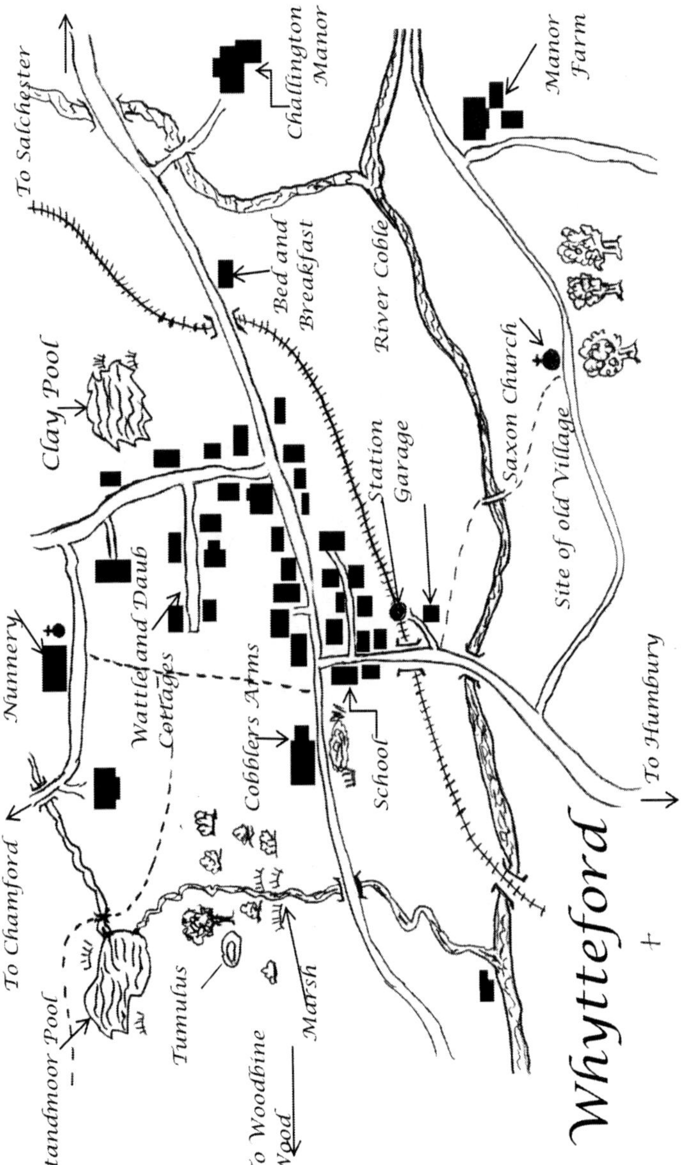
Whytteford
To Salchester
Challington Manor
Manor Farm
Bed and Breakfast
River Coble
Clay Pool
Saxon Church
Station
Garage
Site of old Village
Wattle and Daub Cottages
Nunnery
Cobblers Arms
School
To Humbury
To Chamford
Standmoor Pool
Tumulus
Marsh
To Woodbine Wood

Polish And Polish

When I was about five years old we would visit my grandparents at Chamford from time to time. We travelled on the country bus that followed a twisting route through The Forest. I had learnt to read and signs were usually easy to understand. In one large cleared area there were long huts behind netted fences and there was a bold sign that said POLISH CAMP.

There was a large sign…

I had not noticed this sign until I was able to read and I was unaware of the difference between 'Polish' and 'polish'. I knew what polish was but I had not heard of Poland and Polish people. I read the sign and asked my mother, 'What's a polish camp?' imagining a vast array of shoes about to be made shiny.

'No dear, not polish, Polish,' my mother told me. 'It's a camp for people from Poland.'

No further explanation was given and nothing more was said. I did not discover where Poland was, or why Polish people were living in The Forest, until many more years had passed. If I had been told that the people were Poles my confusion would have known no limits.

It did not cross my young mind that a Polish camp had Polish people and Polish children. After a while the families became integrated into the life of The Forest or they moved away to work in other parts of the country. Several Polish children joined the local school and their English rapidly improved, so much so that despite unusual names that were difficult to spell we forgot that they were Poles and soon knew them as friends.

I became particularly friendly with Tomasz and Patryk who fortunately had names that I could easily pronounce. Tomasz was a little older than me and Patryk was about my age. Best of all they were cheerful boys and they both had a great sense of humour. Their father, who I tried to call Mr Gwozdek, ran a little garage near Whytteford railway station. He sold second-hand cars and also serviced people's vehicles and was well known for his good work.

Visiting Tomasz and Patryk on one occasion I was introduced to Uncle Dougal. How did two boys with Polish names have an uncle named Dougal?

'That's simple,' said Tomasz. 'Our Auntie Karolina married him, he's a Scotsman. We love Uncle Dougal.'

'He's great fun,' said Patryk, 'he always makes us laugh.'

Uncle Dougal was always telling jokes and would sing away as he was working. He drove about The Forest in his little van delivering to remote villages and taking requests for supplies that he would deliver the next week: a teapot for Mrs Hodgson, a set of spanners for Dunbury Farm, a new mallet for Mr Higson or a bridle for young Miss Mattterby's horse. Uncle Dougal could supply anything that was needed and many people were glad of his service as it saved them long trips to Humbury or Salchester.

I was introduced and because nobody told me to do anything else, I always called him Uncle Dougal. In fact most youngsters knew him by that name.

'This is Mark,' said Tomasz.

'Hello, Mark,' said Uncle Dougal. 'I know a quick way of writing your name.'

'How's that, Uncle Dougal?' asked Patryk.

'It's easy. You just do this!' He drew a wiggly line in the dust on the side of his van. 'There,' he said. 'That's a mark!'

'Oh! Uncle Dougal,' said Tomasz, 'don't be so silly!'

We were still using pounds, shillings and pence in those days and if you had a coin worth two shillings and sixpence it was called half a crown.

'Why was the very short clown called Twoandsix?'

'I don't know,' I said starting to giggle.

'Why was he called Twoandsix?' the three of us chorused.

'Because he was only half a clown!'

Mr Gwozdek's business flourished and the little garage became very well known. People from other villages brought their vehicles to him and he was always busy. Sometimes Mr Gwozdek would drive away in his immaculate but elderly Rover to obtain parts that were needed for him to complete some work.

When I was visiting Tomasz and Patryk on one occasion Uncle Dougal was busy at the garage working on his little van.

'Now boys,' said Mr Gwozdek, 'I'm going to Salchester to collect a part for Mr Burman's car. It's been hard to get the part. Tell him I am very sorry but his car won't be ready until tomorrow.'

'What time, Dad?' asked Tomasz.

'I'll have it done by twelve o'clock.'

Mr Gwozdek drove away and Uncle Dougal carried on working on his van. We were entertained by him as joke after joke flowed from his lips. Uncle Dougal was very clever with his voice. He could mimic people and you knew who he was imitating. He could also produce an accent to suit any character.

'Uncle Dougal,' I said. 'How do you do all your funny voices?'

Suddenly he turned into an Italian. 'Whatta you meana bya funee voices, eh bambino?'

'He's been mistaken for a German, a Jew and even a Russian,' said Tomasz.

'He can do animal noises too,' said Patryk.

'Can you?' I asked.

'Mmmooooo!' said Uncle Dougal, sounding like a cow and we all began to laugh.

'Now then, boys,' said Uncle Dougal, 'I've got some fiddly things to do so leave me alone in peace and quiet for a while.'

We went to admire the cars that Mr Gwozdek had for sale.

When Mr Burman arrived, Uncle Dougal could not be seen as his head was tucked under the bonnet of his van.

'Hello,' called Mr Burman.

Tomasz scurried to him.

'Where's your father?' he asked.

'My father is very sorry, Mr Burman,' said Tomasz, 'he had trouble getting a part for your car. It will be ready by twelve o'clock tomorrow.'

Mr Burman looked cross. 'Damned Poles!' he exclaimed.

Uncle Dougal's head slowly emerged from beneath the bonnet of his van.

'Vot is wrong vith us Poles?' he asked.

Uncle Dougal was so convincing that Mr Burman spluttered apologies whilst the three of us sniggered surreptitiously.

'I…I meant no…no…offence…'

'Don't vorry,' said Uncle Dougal. Suddenly he changed his voice to a strong Scottish accent. 'I ken what y'mean.'

Humbury Show

Once a year there was Humbury Show. Officially it was an agricultural show but it included something for everyone. Cattle were on display, as were pigs and sheep, all washed and blow-dried and manicured so that they would look at their best. Horses and ponies were also on show for dressage and performance over jumps. These too were immaculate as were their riders. All of the farm animals were paraded before judges who wore bowler hats. They would huddle together and make notes as proud but anxious owners looked on.

The centre of attention where crowds would gather was the display ring. Here the winning animals were exhibited in front of admiring and applauding crowds. The horses were encouraged over the jumps and the dressage winners strutted around the ring. There were other amusements as well so that all visitors could be entertained.

Although I was very young when I was first taken to Humbury Show I remember it very well. I didn't understand what the horses were meant to be doing but I thought that it all looked very exciting.

The police motorcycle display team were astonishing. At one point eight of them were in formation on one machine. A motorcycle with two passengers in a sidecar came whizzing into the ring. As the machine travelled faster and faster they performed all sorts of tricks, even climbing out and onto the motorbike and exchanging places with the driver. Eventually the sidecar and the machine separated and went in different ways. This both thrilled and terrified me as I didn't realise that everything was very carefully staged.

The band of the County Yeomanry was always a popular feature as they marched, countermarched and played their instruments. Their colourful uniforms looked splendid but the soldiers must have been very hot. I was in awe of the drum major who had an immaculate decorative uniform, gleaming boots and his splendid long silver-topped mace. The reason I was so fascinated by the mace was born through ignorance. All of the musicians were playing their instruments and so I firmly believed that by twirling the mace the drum major caused music to flow forth. How very clever this was!

'I'd love to have one of those twirly things,' I said. But to this day nobody has ever given me one. 'It's wonderful,' I said. 'That man twirls it and music comes pouring out.' Nobody disillusioned me of this fanciful idea and it was some years before I discovered that the wonderful mace was not a musical instrument.

There were not so many cars about when I was young. Most people visited the show on foot or by public transport. Special bus services ran to the show and there were additional trains to Humbury station. When it was time to leave we walked back to the car that my father had hired for a few days. We made our way across the field towards an oak tree under which many cars were parked. I suppose I was rather tired after all the excitement and I lagged behind the rest of the family.

Suddenly I heard my name being called. 'Mark! Mark!' I ran in the direction of the calling voice. But then I was called again. 'Mark! Mark!' This was from another direction and so I ran that way. But then my name was called again. 'Mark! Mark!' This was from the first direction. Then I heard 'Mark! Mark!' and ran that way. Suddenly my father was beside me. I was puzzled. Why had my name been called from different directions? Although I was nearly five years old that was the first time that I had that problem and it was many years before I actually met somebody else with the same name. Although not rare it was not a very popular or fashionable name when I was young.

Eventually Humbury Show gained greater publicity. Television broadcasting had come to the region and a hapless reporter and cameraman were sent to give unsuspecting viewers exciting glimpses of rural delights. The parade of notably blond prize-winning sheep received attention from the camera followed by well-groomed cows that had seldom looked so immaculate.

The reporter moved on to some of the other attractions. There were unusual competitions to be won and so bowling for a pig was featured as was climbing the greasy pole at the top of which was an indignant goose. This was the prize if anyone could climb to the top of the pole and successfully capture the irate bird.

The reporter returned to the activities in the display ring intending to show the antics of the police display team. Unfortunately he was premature as the team were not able to enter the arena. The reason for this was that a huge prize bull had just been paraded and it had been very uncooperative. There were strong men holding two ropes attached to the ring in the bull's nose, but despite their efforts the bull had taken control. The massive brown and cream creature had a wild look in its eyes and it tossed its head ferociously. The two men attempted to keep the ropes taut but the bull's head swung so rapidly that they could not compete with the bovine power. Occasionally the bull would paw the ground and give a loud bellow.

Just after one especially booming bellow the reporter and his cameraman arrived at the side of the ring, set up their equipment and began to broadcast; the reporter stood with his back to barriers. The bull was intrigued by this development and suddenly became relatively placid. The reporter began his broadcast and the bull gently ambled to the side of the ring and positioned himself behind the man holding his microphone as he stared into the camera. The beast was thirsty after all the exertions and stood with its tongue hanging out and saliva dribbled from its mouth. Every now and then the bull lolloped its tongue right round its jaw and would then give a yawn that revealed the state of its teeth and the very depth of its mouth but it remained quiet.

The reporter continued his introduction to the forthcoming police display team. Perhaps the bull felt that it was being ignored as it suddenly gave a lunge to the very edge of the ring and stood right behind the reporter. The giant again released its tongue, and, head pushed forward, released a stream of thick saliva over the hapless reporter's shoulder. Then, to complete its repertoire, the bull gave a bellow that was broadcast throughout several adjacent counties as the poor victim collapsed in front of the camera.

The bull stood right behind the reporter…

A Few Pints Of Milk

You could hear the horse plodding along the lanes every day. His name was Prince and he pulled the green milk float to The Forest villages from the dairy in Humbury. The sound wasn't a crisp clip-clop of hooves on the road. Instead we heard Prince's ponderous progress together with the familiar clink of milk bottles in crates as the deliveries were made. Two pints for Mrs Manners. Four pints for the Bunden family, as they had several children who never seemed to stop growing. They even needed nine pints on Saturdays, especially if Grandma Bunden was staying with them.

You could hear the horse plodding along the lanes…

I used to look out for the big green milk float. Terry Walder was the milkman and his float always gleamed as he polished it every morning before setting out. Prince was well cared for too. The hair around his great hooves was trimmed and his thick mane was neatly cut and well brushed. Terry would spend hours tending his horse, making sure he had the best food and brushing his black coat so that it shone on even the gloomiest days. Prince always looked very distinguished and all the children loved him. Even though he towered over us we never felt frightened of this great carthorse. What was there to frighten us? Nothing at all! Prince's movements were all gentle and if we stood close to him with a few lumps of sugar in our hands he would gently nuzzle us.

'He knows you'm gart summat for'im,' Terry would say as Prince snuffled at our hands. 'Give it to 'im or we'll never get the milk round over.'

In the villages Prince could almost have managed the round on his own. He would make his way along the lanes of Whytteford stopping in exactly the right places every day and Terry would deliver a few pints.

'Good marnin', Mrs Sponder. How many for you today?'

'Just the one please, Terry. But I would like half a dozen large eggs. Make sure they're large now.'

'Big'uns eh? What are you goin' to do with 'em?'

'I'm making cakes for the village fête.'

'Jolly good. These are really fresh. I laid them s'marning!'

'And how's Prince?'

'He's foine. Come and say hello.'

And Mrs Sponder would pop out and make a fuss of the gentle horse, holding a carrot in her hand. She always produced something for him to eat and Prince liked that. He seemed to be very fond of Mrs Sponder and as she made a fuss of him he gently coaxed the food from her hand.

Delivery done Terry moved on to his next customer, about fifty yards along the lane. He'd walk swinging his little hand-crate with six bottles of milk, their foil tops gleaming, and whistled as he went up the path to Ella Landy's cottage. If it was a Thursday, he knew that she should be at home as that was Ella's day off from Challington Manor.

'Good morning, Ella. How many today?'

'Better have two, and again tomorrow but four on Saturday.'

'Four eh? What's special abart Saturday? You've never 'ad four on a Saturday!'

'Matter of the fact family's coming and I want to make a milk jelly. Our Maisie's youngest loves that.'

'What flavour?'

'Orange of course.'

'There now.' He handed over the bottles of milk. 'That'll be three and six for this week.'

Meanwhile Prince would have gently pulled the float along the lane and he would be standing waiting for Terry. If he chatted too long at Ella's cottage, Prince would become impatient. He knew where the next stop would be and he liked that delivery, as it would be time for a rest. Prince would whinny and toss his head for a moment or two until eventually Terry climbed up to his seat on the float then without a word being said Prince would set off.

It was in this part of the round that Prince's hooves could be heard sounding crisper than anywhere else on the Whytteford round. The great horse towed the float up to The Cobblers Arms and there he stopped, right by the old horse trough. Prince would have a drink and then Terry gave him a nosebag full of delicious oats. Prince would stand gently enjoying his lunch and Terry disappeared in to the bar. Officially he was making a delivery but he also enjoyed a break from the round.

'Having one today?' asked the landlord, who already knew the answer.

'Oi think I deserves an'alf,' Terry would say.

'Just a half then?'

'Oi only ever drinks 'arves. Oi never 'as an'ole pint.'

'Very well, a half it shall be.'

'Well…as it's today make it two 'arves. An' put'm in the same glass!'

Eventually, when Prince had long finished his oats, Terry would come smiling from The Cobblers and the milk round continued.

As long as routine was kept, Prince was happy. But if it was interrupted then Prince needed persuasion.

Occasionally Mrs Sponder was not at home and Prince really missed her. Once he came to a halt outside her cottage and refused to move. Terry became quite agitated, as he didn't know what to do. The gentle Prince had suddenly become very stubborn and he refused to budge. And then Terry had a clever idea. He took Prince's nosebag from the back of the milk float and walked up to The Cobblers Arms. At first Prince took no notice. Terry didn't look back but went into the bar.

'Oi think I deserves an 'alf.'

'I didn't hear you coming.'

'Prince is down the road. Oi couldn' wait for 'im.'

'What's happened? Have you two had an argument?'

Suddenly the sound of the great hooves was heard approaching The Cobblers.

'What's that then? Has he followed you?'

'Spec-so. Arter all he knows the round better'n me!'

It was a warm day and the windows were open. Suddenly Prince's great head looked in through the window.'

'He's looking for you. That's what he's doing.'

'It's my guess he's really lookin' for 'is food.' Terry walked to the window and gave prince his nosebag. 'There you are. Now jus' enjoy thart!'

'I see what you mean,' said the landlord.

'Oi think I deserves another 'alf. Oi only ever drinks 'arves. Oi never 'as an'ole pint.'

'Then have this one on the house.'

'Thank'ee. That's moighty good of 'ee.'

'It's not often a horse pokes his head through the window. He could become quite a tourist attraction.'

Don't They Know It's Christmas?

Although Auntie Madge was a difficult person and a deeply unwanted guest, at times there was no escape from her and the selfishness that she spread bounteously wherever she went. At Christmas she would stay with my grandparents at Chamford. This was a few miles away in another part of The Forest but distance did not have any effect on Madge and she could still cast her pall of gloom; blissfully unaware of the despair that followed in her wake. On Christmas Day she would drive them to us and spread her dubious charm around our home.

Madge was married but her husband was a welcome contrast as he was warm and sociable. Geoffrey was always courteous and good humoured despite the cantankerousness of his wife. Madge had been on familiar form when they had arrived one Christmas Day. She snapped at her husband whatever he did, demanding total attention and treating him as if he were her personal servant.

'I need a drink!' she demanded. 'Make sure it's a good one.' This meant that she wanted a gin and dry vermouth without too much vermouth.

Her extravagant tastes were so indulged by Geoffrey that they fortunately brought the necessary bottles with them; two of each to be on the safe side.

Before the first sip had fully passed her lips Madge passed her judgement.

'Too weak!' she declared.

'Easily remedied,' Geoffrey gently replied and he took the offending glass away and topped it up with neat gin.

Content with this enhanced drink Madge decided she should offer some 'help' in the kitchen. As she entered, my father was taking the turkey from the oven. He was always in charge of roasting 'the bird' and took great pride in ensuring that it was perfectly cooked. It sat sizzling from the heat of the oven and was a glorious golden brown.

'What a wonderful sight!' declared Madge, breathing alcohol laden breath over the turkey. 'Oh, you beautiful bird!' she added and she stroked its hot plump breasts. 'Oooh it's hot!' She then took another swig of her drink then looked sorrowfully at the empty glass. 'My glass is empty! We can't have that!' She then opened the door and bellowed, 'Geoffrey, drink!' The kitchen was warm and Madge, already well lubricated, was becoming very rubicund.

'Now what can I do to help?'

'Every thing's fine,' my father replied.

'But I must help. I can't possibly let you good people do all of the work. It wouldn't be fair. I must make my little contribution.'

'Could you go and check on the fire?' suggested my father. 'Make sure it's burning well.'

'Very well! If that's the best I can do!' Madge indignantly swept from the kitchen colliding with Geoffrey who was arriving with another drink. 'As usual you are in the wrong place!' she snapped seizing the glass as she pushed her husband aside.

Eventually it was time for Christmas lunch and as we were all seated at the table my father produced a bottle of wine. This was a treat for a special occasion.

'Only the one bottle?' asked Madge. 'That won't go far.'

'I'm sure you'll cope,' Geoffrey muttered mostly to himself but he nevertheless drew a smile from my father.

As the meal was served Madge demanded, 'Where's the bread sauce?' My father loathed bread sauce and my mother was very happy to follow his wishes. 'Christmas lunch is incomplete without bread sauce.'

'My meal is complete,' Geoffrey said, intending to spread benevolence amongst us all, 'especially in such delightful company.'

'You are easily pleased,' snapped Madge, intending to

crush her husband's kind words.

'I must have been when I—' but he stopped the sentence, not wishing to cause an argument at the lunch table.

'What were you going to say?' snapped Madge.

As I was only six years old at the time I was unaware of all the undercurrents of these conversations. Christmas Day was one of the best days of the year and I always enjoyed every moment of it. There would have been exciting presents to open and enjoy. New books to admire and begin reading. There was the glow of the log fire and the twinkling candles on the Christmas tree that were lit whilst presents were distributed and again in the evening when the excitement was dying down.

Candles on the Christmas tree

After lunch Madge demanded a bed to rest in as she had been 'up late wrapping presents' and was tired. Really the only safe position for her by this time was horizontal and as it meant that she would be out of the way for a couple of hours her wish was quickly accommodated.

Uncle Geoffrey good humouredly came and helped me put new wagons on my railway, read me a story and then reluctantly muttered, 'Better see how the old girl is doing,' and disappeared.

A few moments later I heard raised voices from Madge and Geoffrey. I didn't really react as both tended to speak loudly in each other's company. Madge, because that was her constant manner, and Geoffrey because he was not going to be overwhelmed by his wife. Eventually they left taking my grandparents with them and an aura of calm spread though our festive home.

As I said goodnight to my parents my father asked me a question.

'Have you had a good day?'

'I've had a wonderful day, thank you.'

'Well, I'm glad one of us has.' For some reason I did not comprehend that my father had not enjoyed the day.

I left the room and made my way upstairs with Bob, my teddy bear, who, as always, was smiling contentedly. As I left the room I could hear my parents talking.

'What a day,' said my mother. 'What a day! You'd think they could behave for one day.'

There was a moment of silence and then my father spoke.

'Don't they know it's Christmas?'

A few weeks later Geoffrey heard a sentence that must have been music to his ears. 'I am leaving you!' Madge had declared. 'You restrict me and make my life unbearable.' This was entirely true as he did his best to control his wife's excesses of mood and temper. When Geoffrey heard the dramatic announcement he did not demur. His response was to quietly leave Madge to her self-satisfied indignation and go shopping. He returned an hour or so later with a huge package that he presented to his soon to be ex-wife.

'A final present for you,' he said as he thrust the bundle at Madge. 'Use it well and use it soon.'

'Oh, Geoffrey,' Madge responded, 'please forgive me, I didn't know you cared so much.'

'That shows how much you mean to me.'

Madge ripped off the thick brown paper wrapping and found that her gift was a large suitcase.

'That's just what you need and it is a pleasure to give it to you,' Geoffrey declared, and he never spoke to Madge again.

Cheese Scones

It was summer time and the weather was perfect.

'Let's have a picnic at home,' declared my father. 'The wood is looking wonderful. We'll go down there and have a picnic.'

My mother, always cautious about al fresco dining, agreed and so tea was going to be in the open air. My grandparents were invited and so was ghastly Auntie Madge. We hadn't realised that she was staying with Grandma and Grandpa that weekend and so there was no escape; we would have to suffer her dominating company. Old Harry was also invited as he had been at school with my grandfather.

'Queen will bring us over,' my grandfather declared and our spirits wilted.

We gathered up food, deck chairs and even a picnic table. A huge, ancient but well-starched table cloth was packed into the picnic box together with a kettle, tea, milk and several bottles of beer.

Once my grandparents had arrived with Auntie Madge, some considerable time after they were expected, we ventured down to the wood and 'camped' by the pond. The deck chairs and some rugs were set out, a fire was lit and the kettle, filled with water, was set to boil.

'Take care of the fire,' my mother said to me. 'Make sure you keep it burning well.'

My father opened a bottle of beer. Spying this activity Auntie Madge made a typical comment. 'Oh, you have some beer. Did you bring some gin for me?'

There was a tense silence. As her face was already rubicund from lunchtime drinking it was probably a good thing that none of her favourite tipple was available.

'I thought you would have brought that,' said my father. 'None of us ever drink gin.'

The fire was beginning to burn rather well. I kept

feeding it with dry gorse sticks, it blazed brightly and the ancient blackened kettle obliged by boiling and tea was made.

My grandparents were delighted. Auntie Madge was feeling dissatisfied but she could not do anything. We ate sandwiches and pork pie and my mother had made a delightful Victoria sponge. She also produced a gleaming ginger cake scattered with almonds. Unfortunately Madge had brought her own contribution to the picnic. She opened a tin.

'Would anyone like a cheese scone?' she asked just as my mother was about to offer some of her wonderful creations.

Cheese scones sounded like an excellent contribution to the picnic but surprises were in store for those who accepted them.

'I'll have some sponge,' said Grandma.

'I'll have one, Queen,' said Grandpa who would never offend his darling daughter.

'So will oi,' said Harry.

Grandpa and Harry then fell into a conversation that became more incomprehensible due to the strong Forest dialect as it progressed.

Much to my surprise my father accepted a scone but my mother declared that she really didn't have room for anything else.

'You'll have one, won't you?' said Auntie Madge thrusting the tin of scones in my direction. Her words came not as a suggestion but as a command and so I obediently accepted one of her scones.

I soon realised that I had made a big mistake. Ghastly Auntie Madge was not an expert baker and today she had excelled herself by failing in every respect. Scones are meant to be light and crumbly yet the one I had selected was so solid that it would not have been out of place included in a wall. But that was not the only quality that this creation possessed. Cheese had certainly been included in the recipe but it was so old that it might have been an interesting exhibit in a museum. I struggled with my first bite and was nearly sick when I took a second. I noticed that there was two thirds of a scone left on my grandfather's plate and that Harry's hand had suddenly slipped into his pocket. He produced a huge handkerchief that he used to cover most of his face and then thrust back into his pocket.

What could I do? My cheese scone was revolting and I had struggled to eat any of it. If I ate any more I would be violently sick and that would upset my grandmother who was especially sensitive since she had suffered a stroke some years before. Desperate events can lead to desperate remedies. Suddenly inspiration struck. The fire! I was meant to be in charge of the fire. I hastily went to gather some more dry pieces of gorse, slipped the remains of the revolting scone amongst them and fed the fire, which was soon blazing well. I refilled the kettle with water and placed it on the fire.

'You'll have another of my cheese scones, won't you,' said Auntie Madge thrusting her tin in my direction.

The fire burnt well…

'Yes please,' I said and I noticed that my father looked astonished.

'You haven't finished your scone, Pa,' Auntie Madge said accusingly to my grandfather.

'Oh, ah,' he said, 'bit rich for me.' But under her stern gaze he picked up the rest of his scone and suffered the consequences.

I had no intention of attempting to eat another scone. I went to gather some more dry wood for the fire and slipped the solid creation amongst the pieces of old gorse. Auntie Madge was so busy talking that she didn't notice my activity. I fed the fire and the flames soon consumed my scone as well as the wood. Unfortunately some smoke drifted in my mother's direction.

'There's a peculiar smell from the fire,' she said. 'I wonder what it is.'

Eventually the picnic was over and my grandparents departed with Queen. Harry stayed on for another bottle of beer and the tranquillity of The Forest calmed us down. Why was it that any visit from Auntie Madge was so stressful? She was always dominating and usually unbearable but on this day she had added a new terror with her failed baking.

'Those scones looked awful,' said my mother.

'They were made with cheese that was so stale that mice would have rejected it,' said my father.

'How did you manage to eat two of them?' asked my mother.

'I didn't,' I said.

'But I saw you accept a second one. Did you really like them that much?'

'I ate just two bites from the first scone.'

'Then what did you do with the rest?'

'The fire burnt well, didn't it?' I said.

At that moment there was a sudden bang that came from the fire.

'Whatever caused that bang?' asked my mother,

nervously.

I investigated and found fragments of burnt scone had showered the area around the fire.

'The cheese scone exploded.'

'Then I'm glad you didn't eat it. Just think what might have happened.'

Down At The Station

A railway line from Humbury to Salchester meandered across The Forest and passed through Whytteford. The village was lucky as the station was close to the centre and so it was usually quite busy when a train arrived. Although they were not fast by today's standards the service was reliable and the trains were much quicker than the ancient buses that rattled along the roads and lanes. The trouble with the country bus service was that the driver knew everybody and so the journey was quite a social occasion. As each passenger boarded niceties were exchanged together with a good deal of gossip and news. This meant that on busy days it might be running forty minutes late before it reached the village and by the time I reached Humbury or Hindhurst it could be up to an hour behind schedule.

Whytteford Station was usually a quiet place but when a train arrived there would be a sudden business as parcels were unloaded, baskets of pigeons placed carefully on the platform, crates of produce delivered and even parts for cars that were being repaired at the nearby garage. A few times each day the station seemed to be especially important as trains arrived from opposite directions, passengers alighted and suitcases occasionally littered the platform. Then signals clanked, guards' whistles blew, carriage doors slammed and hands waved as the trains were about to depart. The locomotive whistles would give shrill screams, there would be heavy puffing as one train departed and then the other train would ooze steam and smoke and move off. Peace would then gradually descend as the trains escaped to the distance, red and white semaphore signals on high posts creaked and clanged again and then buzz and excitement was suddenly over.

Really the station was not of great significance but because trains passed it could seem a rather exciting place. The staff pottered about their work and their hobbies at a very gentle pace for much of the day. The Station Master had to keep accounts carefully but he also had time for gardening. The flowerbeds on the platform were always full of colour in the summer. An ancient group of fruit trees grew close to the 'down' platform and provided good crops of eating apples from September onwards. At the signal box the signalman had plenty of time to tend a patch of garden. He was very busy when a train was due and for a few minutes after arrival but then there was time for other activities until the next train arrived. On the few occasions each day that trains passed he might be busy for as long as twenty minutes, checking signals, exchanging tokens and then setting the signals for departure. As this was a single line railway each box had a complicated machine from which tokens like giant keys were taken by the signalman. The token was given to the train driver and then he could proceed. All this was done to ensure that only one train was running on the section of railway at any time.

'Go and buy some tomatoes,' my mother said to me one day.

The nearest shop that sold tomatoes was at Chamford which was a long way to walk and so I was surprised by this instruction.

'From Chamford?' I asked.

'No, from the station.'

'From the station? How can I buy tomatoes at the station?'

'Go and see Reg, he'll sell you some tomatoes. Here's some money.' She passed me a few coins. 'And remember to call him Mr Alder.'

I walked to the village over the bridge and in to the station and on to the platform.

'Hello, young'n,' said the Station Master. 'Where are you going today?'

'I've come for some tomatoes.'

'You want Reg.'

'Is that Mr Alder?'

'That's right, that's Reg. Just walk along the platform and along to the box. There's no train due so you'll be safe.'

The signal box was made of brick and wood that was decorated in green and cream. Reg kept the box looking smart, painting the woodwork between his duties. Close by the box were some garden frames. The weather was warm and as I approached Reg was watering some tomato plants that were loaded with glowing ripe fruits.

Close by the box were some garden frames.

'Good morning, Mr Alder,' I said.

'Now, you call me Reg. I 'ate bein' called Mr Alder. Souns pompuss.'

He had a curious way of speaking often missing out sounds but somehow I understood what he said. Reg finished his watering and then turned to me. 'Now wha' can I do for you?'

'We'd like some tomatoes, please.'

'Where's th'other one then?' He looked to my left and to my right.

'What do you mean?'

'You'm said 'we' would like tomaters. So who's with yer?' He laughed. 'C'mon. Let's see what we can foind.' But at the moment a bell rang in the signal box. Reg ran up the wooden steps into the box, rang a bell and pulled a lever that changed the signal. 'Train coming.'

A few moments later the sounds of a steam locomotive approaching were heard and the train appeared but at first the locomotive could not be seen. This was a push-pull service that was propelled by an elegant Victorian engine. The paintwork was gleaming and the brass and copper shining as the crew were proud of their locomotive; in a few months it would be replaced by a thumping diesel unit. As the train came near the box Reg came down the steps holding something looking like an unstrung tennis racquet and he held it up. What looked like the handle was the token for the next part of the journey. The driver leaned from the locomotive and grasped the token as Reg gathered another token from him. The train stopped and one passenger arrived but nobody boarded. Then with whistling, puffing and clanking the train went on its way.

'Now,' said Reg, 'let's pick some tomaters.'

He produced a brown paper bag and filled it with ripe tomatoes. I reached into my pocket.

'I don'need any money. I've got s'many tomatoes they'll last me till Christmas even if I give'm to Santa.'

'Thank you very much. Mum will be grateful.'

'Don'you tell her about't. Give yersell some extra pocket money!'

He gave me a conspiratorial smile and wink.

'On yer way, now. No trains are due. Yer be safe.'

Sunday Lunch

After my grandmother had a severe stroke our life in The Forest changed. Suddenly her welfare was a major concern. Gradually she improved. Her speech returned, her eyes recovered their twinkle, she laughed again. Grandma could not walk and she was confined to a wheelchair but in a strange way she enjoyed her life. Although she was given exercises and she tried to recover the use of her left leg and arm there was very little progress. There would be no more sewing, knitting and crochet work from Grandma. My grandfather took care of her and gradually their life settled into a gentle rural routine.

Each Sunday my grandfather pushed Grandma to the church at Chamford where they enjoyed the morning service. Afterwards there was always a lot of conversation but eventually they emerged from the crowd to see my father waiting for them with his Land Rover. Grandma was lifted in to a seat and her wheelchair would be stowed in the back where Tim would be waiting, eager to be fussed over by Grandpa. Tim seemed to understand that the visits of my grandparents were good news for him.

On Saturdays the butcher delivered a joint ready for the next day. On one occasion he threw a bone to Tim who immediately grabbed it and retreated to his box to enjoy his booty. Once a bone was between his jaws this normally loving, gentle and placid dog suddenly changed personality. He defended his territory and his treat with ferocious growls. He had an aggressive look in his eyes as he bared his teeth. Even my mother, who Tim adored, was not allowed anywhere near him whilst the bone was in his possession. Eventually when the benefits of the bone had been well savoured and it had been gnawed and sucked Tim abandoned it then calmly capered into the garden and all of us were his friends again.

Sunday lunch for most families is usually a delicious meal with a range of dishes to delight everyone but each time that they visited our lunch menu was dictated by Grandma and Grandpa's personal tastes. The joint had to be well roasted. As grandma was fond of it there was always buttered swede. Mashed potatoes had to be served for Grandpa as well as the roasted ones that he did not eat and there would always be cauliflower, cabbage or sprouts if they were in season. And then there were the dreaded butter beans that had been left to soak in a solution of bicarbonate of soda the night before. This was meant to soften them but for me they still seemed to have a leathery case and I cannot remember that they ever tasted of anything interesting. Often Grandpa had brought fresh peas or beans with him but as he did not pick them until the pods were almost bursting the contents were past their best. My mother cooked them well but she seldom succeeded in making them soft. As Grandpa had grown this produce we had to be grateful and not waste anything. There was not a lot for me to enjoy in this meal as I loathed most brassicas and the 'freshly picked' items were not at all appetising as they took a great deal of chewing.

Perhaps the pudding would be more interesting. My grandmother's favourite desert was steamed canary sponge pudding. Usually this has lemon curd put into the basin before the sponge mixture. But Grandma didn't like lemon curd. Lemon rind and juice should be included in the mixture but Grandma didn't like lemons and so some yellow food colouring was added that I suppose made it look something like a canary sponge pudding but did not add to its anonymous flavour.

'Do we have to have that again?' I would ask whilst it was being prepared.

'It's Grandma's favourite pudding.'

"Well it's not mine!'

'But it's Grandma's.'

'Ah, my favourite,' Grandma would say as the pudding arrived at the table together with a jug of custard. 'Custard too,' she would add on every occasion.

It's Grandma's favourite pudding...

I can't say I enjoyed either of these so called delights and so I would request a small helping of the anonymous pudding and a dribble of custard. Eventually the meal was over and it was time to feed Tim.

Whilst we enjoyed or endured this meal Tim, his tail wagging with excitement, would be waiting patiently outside the kitchen door, looking forward to any scraps of meat from our plates and other remnants of the joint. My father had been brought up on a boring regime of roast meat on Sunday, cold meat on Monday and any remainders minced for a pie on Tuesday; consequently he insisted that our entire joint had to be finished and if there was a little left over then Tim was delighted. The meat and a generous helping of gravy were put on to Tim's tin plate and it was placed on the floor. Tim would stare at my father with pleading eyes until he was told that he could eat. When the nod was given the plate was licked round and round the floor, as Tim enjoyed his Sunday treat, until there was not even a last lick of gravy remaining.

I think that Tim enjoyed those Sunday lunches a lot more than I did!

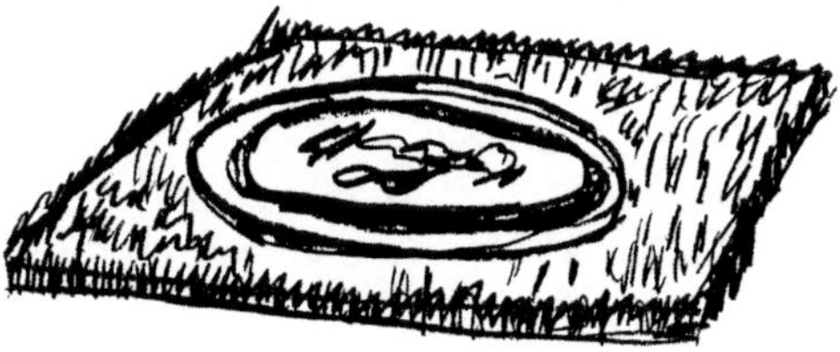

The meat and a generous helping of gravy were put on to Tim's tin plate

Just A Little Fire

The school holidays had arrived. No more lessons, no homework and no more ghastly school lunches for weeks and weeks. No more pointless Maths, grim French, tedious Latin and hateful sessions in the gym. Once the excitement of the first few days of freedom had passed fresh activities began. What should I do? Explore in The Forest? Build a den? Search for deer?

There was plenty of space to build a den and a friend was coming to stay. It would be fun. I gathered branches from round and about and odd pieces of timber left over from various projects. Everything was ready for construction to begin. My friend arrived and we gradually erected a very rustic den. We dug holes, put in poles and tied the timber together with twine. At the end of a day we had a strong structure that just needed covering. The next morning we gathered old sacks and polythene and covered the crude construction. We used a huge string needle and secured everything as well as we could. I suspect most Stone Age people could have built something more effective and durable but we felt rather pleased with our work.

I suspect most Stone Age people could have built something more effective and durable…

'We need a place for a fire'

'That's a good idea. We'll be able to cook sausages over it.'

We cut a space in the grass and then found some old bricks and used them to build a safe base for the fire. We gathered dry kindling wood and newspaper, built the fire then tossed a lighted match into the wigwam of sticks. It was soon alight and the flames were fed with dry gorse.

'That's good. I think a fire always looks friendly.'

'It's burning well.'

'Dead gorse always burns well.'

Pop! Pop! The gorse crackled and popped and sparks flew but not far. Suddenly there was a loud crack from a very dry piece that had ignited. A small chunk of flaming twig jumped from the fire and into some dry grass.

We had failed to take into account that gorse bushes and tussocks of pale, dry grass surrounded our den. The fiery stick landed on a clump and it began to blaze then the flames leapt on to another clump and I dashed off for a can full of water. Too late! The can should have been ready near the fire. The flames flew from clump to tussock and on to tuft after tuft of dry grass. The gentlest of breezes propelled the fire onward. We could not do much but we tried to beat out the flames yet they travelled faster than our feeble beating and spread onwards covering yard after yard. Eventually we knew that nothing we did would make any difference but also saw that nothing needed to be done. The flames did not linger. They passed among bushes and round trees occasionally scorching but never burning. Even the gorse bushes survived almost untouched by the flames. Eventually there was nothing dry for the flames to burn as when they reached fresh moist young grass it would not ignite. Suddenly the fire was over only a few minutes after it had started and all the dead grass had been cleared from at least two acres of woodland.

My friend and I walked up to the house and passed old Harry who was working in the garden.

'That's a roight good'un bit'a work you done this marnin.'

'What do you mean?' I felt that I was going to be in big trouble.

'You'm cleared awl they dead grasses. Now fresh grass can graw. Roight good'un.'

This was not what I expected.

'Oi thinks your'm dad oughter give youm two a whole pound to buy some lollipops!'

I still expected to be told-off but my father was amazingly calm. 'No harm done. Don't worry, just take a bit more care in future.'

But we weren't given a pound to buy some lollipops.

Mother Fox

Mother Fox couldn't understand what was happening. Why was there all this noise? Why were these men so close to her home? Did they know where she lived? What was going on? She peered out from under the bushes watching all the activity but neither of the men seemed to notice her two bright eyes watching them.

A bright yellow beast was close by and the men were talking. What were they saying? All Mother Fox could hear was sounds, she didn't understand their words. Suddenly one of the men pointed right in the direction of her den. What was going to happen? There was a bark. She looked out from under the bush again and saw a black dog standing by one of the men. She'd seen that dog before. He never bothered her, as he was more interested in human beings than animals, but he might catch her scent and show the men where she was. That would never do. Which way was the wind blowing? She sniffed the air. The wind was taking her scent away from the men and the black dog. She could keep watching.

'I want a long ditch,' a man was saying, 'right across here.' Mother Fox still did not know what was going on but she realised that the man was pointing towards her again and across the field and further away.

'How deep?'

'About three feet.'

'That's fine. It shouldn't take too long. The soil here's very sandy.'

'It is on the top, but it gets much harder further down. Almost like soft stone.'

'I can break it up if I have to.'

'I'll leave you to it, then.'

The man who'd been pointing walked away and the black dog stretched himself then trotted after him. Mother Fox watched as the other man climbed up on to the seat of the big machine. There was a great growling sound and the yellow beast roared and puffed smoke. The monster made some funny clanking noises that Mother Fox did not like and it began moving towards her. Mother Fox felt nervous and retreated deep into the gorse bushes. She didn't want to be near this dangerous creature and so she slipped silently away.

Mother Fox didn't want to be near this dangerous creature…

To the humans and that horrible roaring yellow creature Mother Fox was invisible and that's how she remained. She softly padded along amongst some trees, through long grass and behind a hedge. What was going on? Why was that huge beast so close to her home? She caught a whiff of its blue-grey smoke. Did it have fire in its belly? Was it smoke? It smelt different from smoke. The fumes were foul. Mother Fox thought that the monster was puffing out poisoned smoke and she didn't like it.

From the hedge the vixen watched in fear as the beast stretched out its long neck and then its mouth opened. What a terrible mouth! It was so big, it gaped very wide and it had enormous, vicious teeth. Suddenly the vicious looking head moved down to the ground and tore at the turf, ripping up great clods then tossing them to one side. On and on the creature went. Why was it doing this? It seemed to be biting at the ground, gathering up huge mouthfuls and then spitting them out again. The brutal beast bit deeper and deeper into the soil but it never ate for long. There were some more clanking sounds and the machine lifted its head high, it seemed to look to the left and the right, and then it moved a short distance and began biting deep into the soil again. Mother Fox was certain that she hadn't been seen, but would the creature spy her den and destroy it?

The monster continued to puff foul fumes, raise its jaw and then plunge and tear at the soil. Its head would disappear into the long hole that it was making and then rise high as it spewed out earth. Its vicious jaws and mighty teeth grasped at bushes, bracken, heather and gorse; tearing everything from the ground and Mother Fox watched in terrified awe. Again this vile beast moved on and tore at the ground close, oh so close, to Mother Fox's home. She was distraught. Early in the morning she had left her three cubs in the den and gone hunting for unwary rabbits. She had returned, later than intended, with a fresh rabbit in her jaw. It was then that she had encountered the yellow fiend that was attacking the ground. The destruction lasted for ages and the brute kept moving on. Mother Fox was sure its jaws had torn soil from the walls of her den and probably terrified her cubs. It may have attacked them or even have crushed them to death. All Mother Fox could do was watch and hope.

The evil brute stopped roaring so loudly and moved away puffing noxious fumes as it went. The man with the black dog walked back and viewed the destruction then left the scene not knowing that two alert but worried eyes followed every move. As soon as they were out of sight Mother Fox emerged from the hedge. It was late afternoon and the sun was still bright and warm but she had to search for her cubs. There was no sign of other humans so she ran swiftly across the grass and heather to the devastation close to her home. All of the entrances were blocked with soil that the monster had crudely released from its jaws. Mother Fox began to dig the sandy earth using her front paws to throw it out behind her. Fortunately the digging was easy but there was a lot to move. She didn't look around to see if she was being watched, she just dug and dug. Mother Fox began to tire. There was so much earth to move and she had no help. The pile behind her rose high and she kept on digging, determination overcoming her tiredness. She was creating a tunnel through the soil that would lead to her three cubs. Suddenly the earth gave way beneath her front paws. She had done it! Mother Fox sniffed into the dark and could smell them. She called softly and heard little whimpers. They were alive but were they safe? She crawled in through the hole and smelt each cub. There was no scent of blood.

Gently Mother Fox lifted a cub in her mouth and took it from the earth and left it to rest under the bush where she had hidden when her torment began. She did this twice more and then rested. Her task was nearly complete but she was tired. Nearby there was an old rabbit warren where they could hide for the night. When she was ready she would take her cubs there and feed them. The carcass of the rabbit she had caught at the beginning of the day was under a bush. There would be enough food for her cubs. Once they were fed Mother Fox would have to go hunting again.

Trouble With Mice

My mother loathed mice and all other rodents. She detested them to such an extent that the words 'mouse' and 'mice' were never uttered. A birthday or Christmas card that featured a mouse was unwelcome and rapidly discarded. If the sender asked, 'Did you like my card?' she replied, 'Thank you for sending it. That was very kind of you.' My mother could not accept that such creatures existed for a purpose; to her they were unnecessary and she abhorred them. Owls were regarded as wonderful birds as they searched for rodents but she preferred not to realise how the prey was consumed. Even squirrels were treated with suspicion, especially after she encountered one rattling the letter box at the front door and lifting the flap as if it were trying to squeeze through and enter our home. When mice actually invaded our house Mother regarded it as a crisis of biblical proportions.

It happened just after my parents had gone to bed. My father was semi-asleep and my mother was reading a novel. She was concentrating on the story and my father, wholly relaxed, was enjoying the delicious moments between being awake and being asleep. Those seconds when life seems perfect and nothing can trouble, concern or upset you. He was probably just on the verge of slumber, his first snore, when a mouse ran across the carpet. My mother, sensing a movement, looked up as the mouse disappeared beneath a door.

A mouse ran across the carpet…

'A mouse!' she shrieked and jabbed my father with a pointed elbow.

My father, who a moment before had been in a peaceful world of his own, awoke and was suddenly sitting upright. This was a surprise for him as his brain told him that he was horizontal.

'What?...Wh...at?' he spluttered.

'A mouse has just run across the room! Do something!'

'What?...Wh...at?'

Father went to find mouse traps and when he returned my mother was upright on the bed trying to pull off the sheets and blankets that she was standing on.

'What the blazes are you doing?'

'I'm not sleeping in this room whilst there are mice about!'

'But it's already gone.'

'We're sleeping in the spare room.'

The spare-room bed was made up, mother tried to settle down, traps were set and no further disturbance was endured. Father, always able to fall asleep in a moment, was soon snoozing contentedly. Mother was determined not to sleep and was on 'mouse watch' until her eyes closed. Next morning, when he awoke, my father was puzzled to find himself in a different bed and a different room. He remembered very little of the nocturnal escapade until he found two occupied mouse traps.

How had the mice entered the house and reached upstairs? This was a puzzle. Traps were placed in strategic positions where mice might roam. No more little creatures were captured and so it was assumed that the problem was over.

A few days later Auntie Madge announced that she was coming to stay. She hadn't been invited but she informed us of her plans. The dreadful Madge had an air of self-superiority probably because her father had regarded her as his little queen and continued to call her 'Queen' for the rest of his life. Spoilt as a child, and still spoilt as an adult, she expected everybody to succumb to her wishes and it was easier to accede than fight; otherwise there would be a tantrum. To say that she was not welcome would be an understatement and the forthcoming visit created a feeling of impending doom that permeated the house and spread gloominess throughout the family.

'I'll be with you in time for tea,' Madge had declared and she duly arrived over two hours late.

'We've been waiting for you.'

'I spend my working life doing things by a certain time. When I am away from work a clock is not going to dictate when I do things.' Madge was being herself.

'But we needed our tea.'

'Well I said I'd be with you at tea time and I am here so it is tea time.'

My mother went to boil the kettle and my father was disappointed when she said that she didn't need any help. The evening passed and eventually Madge declared that she was off to bed and we all heaved a collective silent sigh of relief as the dominating presence left the room. Little did we know what was about to happen.

Suddenly there was an ear-piercing shriek from upstairs. We dashed to the hall and looked up the stairs and were confronted by an alarming vision. There was Madge in a voluminous nightgown, her hair infested with curlers and her face smothered in a beauty cream that was certainly failing to do its job.

'A mouse is in my bedroom!' Madge declared. 'I cannot stay in a house that has a *plague* of mice running about all over the place. One might attack me in the night! I am leaving.' She disappeared into the bedroom.

A smile of delight gently spread over my father's face, he looked at my mother and she began to smile.

Meanwhile Madge was making a lot of noise in her bedroom as she hastily packed her things. The door then flew open and Madge, her head still engulfed with curlers, burst forth with an overcoat over her night attire. Full of indignation she strutted down the stairs and out through the front door.

'I shall never stay in this unhygienic, rodent-infested, pest-ridden and verminous house ever again!'

Next day my father, puzzled as to how another mouse had crept into our home, began his investigation. Some years previously he had planted a cotoneaster against an outside wall. It had grown strongly upward until it was pressing under the low eaves. Our home had rooms in the roof with dormer windows. That autumn the mice must have climbed the cotoneaster, enjoyed eating the berries and then carried on up and along the twisting stem, found a small gap and crept into the house. The bush was cut back severely and we never had the problem again.

'It was a nasty episode,' said my father, 'but not without benefit.'

'What do you mean?' asked my mother.

'Well, Madge has said she will never stay here again.'

My mother mused for a moment, relishing the thought. 'I still don't like mice,' she said, 'but perhaps, after all, they do have their uses!'

This Way And That

Every day the little van meandered through the villages. The engine rattled as it came to a stop outside a cottage then a rotund but nimble figure would pop from the van and shove a newspaper into an old pipe hanging by the gateway. He'd slip back into the van and the engine would reverberate and rattle as it pulled away, clattered a distance along the lane, lurched to the other side then stopped again.

Very early each morning Gideon Strang drove to Humbury station and collected a stack of newspapers. Mouthing the names of his customers he'd sort them into piles for each village.

'Mrs Sponder, Telegraph; Colonel Bassett, Times; Edna, Mirror.' Gideon held the lists in his head. 'Jeb, Express; Rector, Telegraph; Joe Gramble, away.' He rattled through the lists and in a few minutes the stacks were ready to be put in his van. 'Chamford, Whytteford, Breamhill, Brookford and off we go.'

'Chamford first today.' Gideon varied his round trying to keep customers happy. The van's engine whined with a unique note and the rattling never stopped. Suddenly it would soften as Gideon pulled in to one side of a lane and made a delivery. Then the engine jangled, the hidden tambourine under the bonnet shook more loudly, and it moved off.

'Look out for Gideon...'

'Look out for Gideon!' was often said to drivers on lanes of The Forest. Gideon seldom looked in his mirrors, knew where the next delivery was, and headed to it by the most direct route. He'd swerve across the road regardless of any other vehicles and then veer back again. Sometimes he had to travel as much as a quarter of a mile between cottages, and only then could you be sure that the van would be on the proper side of the road. If all his customers lived to one side of a lane then Gideon's van progressed slowly regardless of traffic regulations. But if one customer – yes, just one customer – lived on the opposite side then the van would career awkwardly across, then, delivery made, it would hurtle back.

Every week he'd call in for payment and often we'd offer him a cup of coffee.

'You must know the roads round here as if there was a map in your head.'

'Reckon you'm muss be roight.'

'How long have you been delivering papers?'

'Since I was a nipper. Used to go round on me boike with a little tray-ler behind him.' Gideon always stretched some words when he spoke.

'So when did you have a van?'

'Bought mee first in 1932. Been driving ever since. T'was a little Aus-tin. Good little runner.'

'1932. So you've been driving for nearly forty years.'

'I expect you find the roads busy today.'

'I do. When I began I could go for miles and nev-er, ev-er see another vee-hick-le. Now they'm all over the lanes.'

The year of 1932 might not seem significant but actually Gideon's revelation explained a lot about his driving skills. The Driving Test was introduced in 1934.

'Never taken the Driving Test.' He seemed almost

proud of this achievement. 'What's more I don't want to.'

'Why's that?'

'I don't think I'd ev-er pass.'

We didn't disagree.

'Business going well, then?' asked my father.

'Ticking along.'

'But does it grow at all?'

'Pretty constant but I wonder about tel-ee-vis-ion.'

'Why's that?'

'There's so much news on tel-ee-vis-ion.'

'Is there now?'

'I expect you see it. Will people want newspapers and tel-ee-vis-ion?'

'That's a good point.'

'What do you think of the news on tel-ee-vis-ion?'

'We've never seen it. We haven't got one.'

'You haven't got a tel-ee-vis-ion? I thought you'm had a tel-ee-vis-ion.'

Although television was quite common in cities when I was young it was not available in many places and was relatively new to The Forest.

'Why haven't you'm got a tel-ee-vis-ion?'

'We're too busy,' said my father.

'Have you got a television, Gideon?' asked my mother.

'Well, we 'as and we 'asn't?'

'Now then, Gideon,' said my mother, who was always very precise. 'You either have a television or you don't.'

'Well then, you'll see what I mean. We have got a tel-ee-vis-ion.'

'So you have got one.'

'Sort of. You see although we have a tel-ee-vis-ion we've not got a picture. It doesn't work. We've only got sound coming from the tel-ee-vis-ion. So as I say, we have a tel-ee-vis-ion and we hasn't got a tel-ee-vis-ion!'

Have Some Ginger Beer…

It all began when we were given a ginger beer plant. I'd never seen a plant like this. It sat in a jar of cloudy liquid looking like a pile of sludge. We fed it with sugar and ginger each day but it never grew any leaves nor did it seem to change. Feeding was the easy part. After a week the hard work began. My brother carefully opened the big jar.

The ginger beer plant was kept in a big jar…

'Pooh, what's that?' A curious smell wafted round the kitchen. 'It smells like something that's been trodden…'

'That's enough!' said our mother.

'Get squeezing,' commanded my brother as three lemons, each halved were thrust in my direction.

I strained to squeeze every drop of juice from the lemons then poured it into a bowl. Their acid scent added to the unique smell from the plant.

'Sugar next.' Three cups of glistening sugar crystals cascaded into the bowl.

'Now some boiling water. Five cups of it.'

I kept well away from the boiling water as it was added.

'Get stirring.'

'Who's making this ginger beer?'

'I am.'

'Then why am I doing all this stirring?'

'Because I'm reading the recipe.'

'I can read too.'

'Be quiet.'

I stirred and stirred, first one way and then for amusement I reversed the motion.

'That's not the way to stir.'

'This is my way.'

'Is that sugar dissolved?'

'I don't know.'

'Let me do it. I'll do it properly.' Older brothers always think they are right.

'What's next?'

'Twelve cups of cold water. You can get those, I'll keep stirring.'

'You'd better use a bigger bowl,' said our mother, producing a large earthenware bowl from a cupboard. We were honoured as this bowl was usually reserved for cake making.

Now came the exciting part of the ginger beer production. The liquid from the plant was added to the concoction in the big bowl. We had been told it had to be strained through muslin.

'What's muslin?'

'I'll use a hanky.'

'I hope it's a clean one. We don't want any funny things in the ginger beer.'

At last the work was done. A big jug was used and we carefully poured the fluid into strong bottles and screwed on stoppers. We made space in the coal shed as we had been told to store them somewhere cool and dark.

'When can we taste it?'

'We will have to wait seven days.'

My brother then had the gruesome job of separating the curiously gooey ginger beer plant. He was keen to have plenty of ginger beer and so he didn't throw anything away. Instead he decided to have another plant.

'This will add to the grocery bill,' our mother declared. 'Six lemons and a bag of sugar each week.'

Eventually a week passed and our first batch of ginger beer was ready for tasting. It had rested quietly in the dark and as it did so something had happened.

We opened the first bottle and heard a satisfying pop as the gas from the ginger beer escaped. The fizzy, pale grey liquid bubbled from the bottle and we sniffed the gingery smell that wafted about.

'That's good,' declared my brother as he sipped from his glass.

'But you've got some work to do,' said our father.

The whole process of ginger beer making was repeated. My arm was tired after double the work of stirring. As we moved round the house we could not escape the smell of the ginger beer. We hunted everywhere until we found enough bottles for the first big batch. Seven days later we hadn't quite finished drinking our first week's creation. The second lot was ready for drinking, but we were struggling to consume all the ginger beer that was produced.

Another problem was the plant. We had to halve it each week and then the feeding began again. We saw the brown sticky pile in the bottom of each jar grow in the cloudy liquid.

'Would you like a ginger beer plant?' we asked our guests.

Eventually most of the homes in Whytteford must have owned one until nobody needed a ginger beer plant. Years before our parents had begun to make marrow rum but they never completed the recipe. The bottles were lurking in the back of the garage. Father rediscovered them and added the sticky, gingery goo. We then forgot about the marrow rum for a few years.

Summer sun warmed the air. Everyone was thirsty. Visitors were all offered a glass of ginger beer and most readily accepted. It was cool and refreshing because the coal shed was always in the shade. But the warmth of the summer speeded up the final stage of production.

'Let's have tea in the garden.'

We carried out chairs and a table and sat in the shade of the apple tree.

The egg sandwiches looked very inviting, red tomatoes glistened amidst fresh lettuce and watercress. Best of all a newly baked cake sat in the middle of the table. Frayed tempers eased as we ate and drank refreshing ginger beer.

The evening sun beat down on the garden but we were in the shade. Calmness and tranquillity spread over The Forest and hung in the air.

Bang!

'What the hell was that?'

'It came from the coal shed!'

''The ginger beer!'

As the effervescence built up in the bottles so did the pressure. For safety it's best to open each bottle daily. When we remembered to do this we enjoyed the hiss as the stoppers were released. The louder the hiss the fizzier the content. Enjoying the summer weather we had forgotten about this safety precaution and in the warmth the bubbling pressure had been building up for some time.

'Quick! Let the gas out!'

With hisses and bubbling the gas was released from the other bottles; often just in time as ginger beer escaped, flooded our hands and dribbled to the ground.

Tim, being an inquisitive dog, sniffed, had a few licks and then made himself comfortable well away from the coal shed. No ginger beer for him.

The birds stopped singing during the day. Foxes stayed below ground, rabbits hid until dusk and the deer retreated deep into woodlands. The heat had silenced the wild life of The Forest. Even the bees buzzed lazily as they gathered nectar.

Gideon's van still rattled along the lanes and so we always knew when he was close with the newspapers. By ten o'clock each morning the sun was baking the paths to every cottage. Gideon arrived with his face glowing brightly and a handkerchief knotted over his head.

'Would you like some ginger beer, Gideon?'

'Ah. That would be champion!' He seized the glass and a few gulps later it was gone.

'Would you like some more?'

'Ah, that I would. 'Tis thirsty work these days.'

We had not realised that homemade ginger beer is mildly alcoholic. The fizziness is caused by natural fermentation. Gideon was teetotal. He'd never drunk anything other than water, tea, coffee and lemonade.

''Tis roight good ginger beer.'

'Have another glass. We've made plenty of it and we'll be making some more soon.'

'Well, as you'm arffered…'

Gideon tossed another glass down his throat.' I noticed that despite cool drinks Gideon's face was redder than when he had arrived.

'Ta very much. Better be on me way. Thanks vereemuch!' Gideon was so cheerful and he pumped our hands vigorously as he bade farewell. And he was off, his little van swerving from one side of the road to the other with even more recklessness than usual.

'What's got into him?' asked our mother.

'Ginger beer,' said our father. 'He's not used to it!'

The Village Bakery

The bakery at Chamford was well established and was of necessity still using a traditional wood-fired bread oven. The lining of heat-retaining bricks was the secret of its success. A wood fire from bone dry sticks was built inside the oven. The fire burnt brightly and strongly, heating the heavy oven walls that absorbed the heat. The fire was built up until the oven was white hot then it was allowed to die down. The oven retained all the heat and the ashes were quickly swept out then the risen loaves of dough were placed in the oven with a wooden paddle. Soon the bakery was filled with the aroma of hot freshly baked bread. Many villages had bakeries like this. The dough was prepared each evening and by early the next day it had risen in the bread tins. Each morning the baker had to be up early to set the fire burning and bake the bread for the day.

Tin loaves and granary loaves…

Eventually the traditional ovens gave way to solid electrical bread ovens that could quickly reach the essential high temperature. The baker still had to rise early to bake the loaves for the day. At Chamford Bakery you could buy cottage loaves of white bread. These always had dark crunchy crusty tops and soft centres. You could tear the loaves in two then cut them into wedges that were perfect for eating with hot soups made from local vegetables. Wholemeal loaves were a tempting bronzed brown with a few baked wheat seeds scattered on the top crust. Some people would only buy white tin loaves so called because the shape of the loaf was dictated by the size of tin in which the bread had been baked. Granary loaves were also spread along the shelves together with cob rolls, floury baps and little wholemeal cottage rolls that children found irresistible.

As well as the various breads, often still warm if you went to the bakery in the morning, there were other delights to be savoured. Chelsea buns rolled with dried fruits and baked bronze adorned the shelves together with shining glossy lardy cakes, buns topped with gleaming icing and sugared ring doughnuts together with others shaped like spongey balls with jam oozing from them. The products of the bakery looked good, smelt appealing and because they were all so fresh tasted delicious. Often you could be eating a still-warm delight from the bakery with hot coffee brewed when you returned home. Many a bun or cake never reached home as they were eaten outside the bakery in a car, in a van or whilst riding a horse or bicycle along a forest road.

On the counter of the Chamford Bakery was a pile of tissue paper and another of crisp white paper bags. Each loaf that was bought was wrapped in the paper; buns, cakes and rolls were slipped into bags. Martha always seemed to be behind the counter whenever the shop was visited. Once each item was wrapped she would write down the price on a little pad kept by the till, add up the cost of all you had chosen and present you with your bill. Martha would add up so quickly that it was a job to keep up with her but she was never wrong. The amazing thing was that she also carried on a conversation at the same time.

'Good morning.'

'Hello, Martha. Two small wholemeal please.'

'Three and six. How's your son?'

'He's fine. Two Chelsea buns.'

'And your husband? Haven't seen him for a while. Two shillings.'

'He's been busy on the farm. Three iced buns, please.'

'Is the harvest good? Three and nine.'

'Pretty good. I'll take a cottage too.'

'It's a busy time of the year. Three shillings.'

'That's all for today.'

'That's twelve and three pence. Fifteen shillings. Thank you. Here's two and nine change.'

'Thank you. See you on Saturday. Will you save me two cottages and a large wholemeal?'

'Certainly, I'll make a note.' Then Martha would turn to the next customer. 'Good morning. I've saved that lardy cake for you.'

Visiting the bakery one Saturday my mother was pleased to see that five wholemeal loaves were sitting on the shelf, ready for her to make her choice. She saw that the rector was already buying some buns.

'Thank you, Martha,' he said as she wrapped the buns in a white bag. 'And I'll take those five wholemeal loaves as well and pop them in the freezer.'

'I'll take those five wholemeal loaves...'

My mother was quietly rather cross but humour took over. She smiled at the man of God and said, 'He'd like two fishes as well!'

Holiday Time

A year after Tim joined our family we went away on holiday. We had no vehicle of our own and so my father hired a car. We took a lot of luggage with us as we were going to be away for two weeks. This was carefully packed into the boot of the car but we could not close it and so a waterproof sheet covered our cases. My mother always started a 'holiday box' of food and would gradually add cans of essentials and breakfast cereals to the box so that when we went away we were well stocked. With so much to load into the car there was no room for Tim.

We had arranged for Tim to stay at home and Mr and Mrs Snodgrove would look after him. The Snodgroves were a genial couple of advanced years. They stayed in our home whilst we were away and although they had not travelled far they said they would be having a holiday as well. I really don't remember much about them except that Mr Snodgrove, usually referred to as 'Old Snoddy', had an unusually large nose but contrarily he had no sense of smell. They came for tea the night before we went away and at the end of the meal Mrs Snodgrove, having finished her bread and jam, licked each of her fingers slowly and methodically in front of everyone.

'Yerm dawg'll be foine,' Snoddy assured us and off we went on holiday.

We set off for the West Country at a very early hour and eventually reached a farm where we were renting a caravan. The roads were very quiet most of the time but on Saturdays in the summer some routes were busy as in those days nearly everybody travelled or returned from a holiday on a Saturday. The railways ran special summer trains that were all pulled by wonderful steam locomotives. The West Country then abounded in many rural branch lines to exciting places like Bude, Bideford, Barnstaple, Buddleigh Salterton and Ilfracombe. These names simply evoked a feeling of holidays. The trains were often worked by Victorian steam engines that were both stylish and delightful. My brother collected railway tickets so we would call in at picturesque stations for him to purchase a souvenir. At one station he was sold the very last ticket in the rack that bore the words 'Southern Railway' even though that company had ceased to exist nearly a decade beforehand.

One place we liked visiting was a quiet spot beneath a huge railway viaduct. We would park the car then extract the picnic items from the boot. A treat whilst we were on holiday was that we were allowed to buy bottles of fizzy drinks. I usually chose cherryade, mainly because I liked the colour. I have no memory of its flavour and I doubt if it really tasted of cherries.

There were other flavours including lime that was an especially lurid colour and orange that almost glowed as it was so bright. My brother once bought a bottle of dandelion and burdock the very name of which I found off-putting. We'd set out deckchairs and camping stools and enjoy our food and drink whilst watching huge trains cross the viaduct bridging the valley. Slow freight trains could be heard approaching some minutes before we could see them and the drivers always responded when we waved. Expresses shot through speeding further in to the West Country.

We visited the seaside resorts with those exciting holiday sounding names. In those days you could park a car easily and there was never any charge. Every resort had its own little station on long twisting single railway lines that reached deep into the West Country and the trains were busy as the holiday makers, never known as tourists, explored the area. On a Saturday it could take half an hour for a train to be unloaded at a resort terminus. As well as the people there were cases galore, pushchairs and prams. Elderly relatives had to be woken and extricated from their seats and then each family would set off in a procession to the place where they were staying. On one occasion the guard of a departing train waved his flag and blew his whistle and the train left without him as he could not fight his way through the passengers and luggage from a train that had arrived twenty minutes beforehand.

Some days we were taken to quiet coves with sandy beaches. Often only a few people were there and occasionally we were on our own. Our father would set everything out, spread out a blanket and much to our mother's despair roll his jacket into a pillow and in a few minutes he would be sound asleep. We enjoyed the sand and the sea although knitted swimming trunks were not the most wonderful of garments as they held the water and even when sopping wet seemed to be very itchy. Even if nobody else was in sight we had to change with towels wrapped round us in case anyone who was nearby saw something that they shouldn't. This was quite a feat and somewhat precarious as a lot of the actions needed meant standing on one leg.

Eventually the holiday drew to a close. Shops had ghastly signs in them saying 'BACK TO SCHOOL' in over-large letters. Why did we have to be reminded that this tedium was looming on time's horizon? The car was re-loaded, another early start was made and we journeyed home.

There was one joy to which we all looked forward; we would soon be seeing Tim again. We knew that he would be so pleased to see us, his eyes would light up and his tail would wag and he would smother us with affection.

The reality was very different. We reached home, thanked Mr and Mrs Snodgrove for taking care of Tim and our house and called to our dear friend who was outside in the garden. We called and called. We went out to him and tried to make a fuss but he turned away from us; we were in disgrace and he wanted to make it plain that by going away we had let him down. Tim had been given to us by people who had allowed him to dominate them. In contrast my father had quickly shown him that he had to behave. He became an obedient and loveable friend but he did not expect to be neglected or left in the care of strangers.

For several days Tim ate the food that we provided and would then disappear and have a snooze well away from us. After a week he was quite friendly and when a fortnight had passed he was his usual tail-wagging self. Never again did we go away without him as we did not want to be in disgrace again. By the time of our next holiday my father had bought a Land Rover and Tim rode in the back, sniffing the air and enjoying every holiday adventure.

Tim rode in the back…

A Spate Of Burglaries

Perkins, the eccentrically-run hardware and ironmongers in Humbury was always an entertaining place to visit. Davey Perkins had a unique and unconventional style of service. If you asked for something that Davey had tucked away on an obscure shelf then he flapped his hands vaguely in the direction of where the item might be and you would be expected to find whatever you wanted yourself. There was always cheerful chatter between staff and customers as well as serious advice about how to use a mole trap or when it was best to bottle fruits.

During a long hot summer Davey benefited from a lot of business. Deckchairs and sunshades sold out. Paddling pools vanished as soon as stock arrived and even Davey's display of watering cans disappeared. But as the hot weather went on and on sales declined. All the cans and garden chairs that people wanted had been bought and there was nothing else that Davey could sell to his summer-loving customers. They were not interested in redecorating sitting rooms or retiling bathrooms and kitchens. Gardening was minimal as grass had turned creamy beige and barely grew; even the weeds shrivelled and died. Davey became worried as the sunny days went on and on and visitors to his shop were few and far between.

There was no sign of this spectacular sunny weather coming to an end. Eventually Davey had to tell Monty, his young assistant, that there would be no work for him.

'I'm sorry, Monty,' explained Davey, 'if the shop's not getting enough business, I can't afford to pay you. This will be your last week.' Davey was really upset as he was wondering how he would manage without Monty who knew where things were better than he did.

'Don't worry, Mr Perkins,' said Monty. 'I understand. Perhaps there will be more business by the end of this week.'

'I doubt it,' said Davey. 'There's no sign of any change in the weather.'

'You never know,' said Monty. 'You never know.'

The next day a few people discovered that odds and ends were missing from their homes and business at Perkins began to pick up. Three people visited and bought window locks and two door chains were sold as well.

Monty served two elderly ladies and advised them about security matters.

'Have you had a problem?' he would ask.

'Somebody has taken my best scissors and my red purse. Fortunately there was nothing in the purse,' explained Mrs Parslee.

'Well some extra security is just what you need. Remember to lock your doors and windows. This hot weather is a burglar's perfect opportunity.'

Each day more customers arrived looking for security equipment.

'My chainsaw's missing. I always leave it in the same place. It's not there.'

'I think you'll need a strong padlock and these window locks might be fitted too.' And the sale of a padlock and several window locks was included in the day's takings.

Many people could not find important things that they had always kept in the same places. Cans of food, wooden steps, garden tools, buckets, purses and even the occasional handbag went missing.

'There's a spate of burglaries round the villages near Humbury and in the town too,' was a much repeated sentence.

'I'll have to improve my locks.'

'Good idea. Young Monty is very helpful. He knows just what you'll need.'

Monty was indeed very obliging. 'I think you need a

better lock,' he'd recommend. 'If you like I'll come and fit it for you.' The less competent at home maintenance were delighted to accept this offer and Monty enjoyed the work as well as the cash he was paid for his efforts. He could quickly nip from one village to another as he was a speedy cyclist.

'Goodness me,' said Davey a few days later, 'business has picked up. Monty, I think I can keep you on for another week.'

'Thank you, Mr Perkins,' said Monty. 'I am very grateful.'

Over the weekend there were some more minor burglaries. A new garden chair was suddenly missing from one cottage.

'I just went in for a cup of tea,' explained the owner, 'and when I came out again it was there, gone!'

'An opportunistic thief,' explained Monty, 'you need to improve your security.'

The evening that the Humbury bowls team met for their weekly practice another string of burglaries occurred. Nothing very valuable was stolen. Some apples vanished from one home, a drill from another, a small radio was removed from a window sill, a couple of bottles of wine slipped from a kitchen store and a whole new bottle of gin disappeared from a drinks cabinet.

The next day Perkins was especially busy as members of the bowls team descended upon the shop and bought a variety of security items. Everybody told Monty what had happened and asked for his advice. Locks and padlocks were sold in abundance that morning. Window locks were also very popular.

'They can be a fiddle to fit,' explained Monty. 'Would you like me to pop round and fix it for you.'

'That's so kind of you, Monty.'

'I'll be round at about half past six, if that suits.'

Of course any time Monty suggested suited very well and ladies of a certain age were delighted to have an efficient and rather handsome young man calling in to help them.

The hot summer continued. The spate of burglaries went on and Monty was kept very busy fitting chains, window locks, second locks on ancient doors and security to sheds, garages and out buildings that had never had any security at all.

'You need to improve your security…'

When the weather changed the good citizens of Humbury and the surrounding villages returned to life's routines and made intriguing discoveries. The missing apples were found on a high shelf but were no longer fit for consumption; the bottles of wine were tucked into the wrong cupboard. The gin was found among the cleansers under the sink. A mower was in the wrong outhouse. The radio was on a table in a rarely used bedroom. The red purse was in a different handbag. The scissors were found in a bottom drawer instead of being with the rest of the cutlery. The chainsaw was under a tarpaulin covering a wheelbarrow that hadn't been used for weeks because it wasn't needed. Wooden steps were resting up in the rafters of an outhouse instead of leaning against a wall. The drill was hidden underneath some old sacking. Handbags were suddenly discovered in the 'wrong' wardrobe. The missing cans of food were at the back of cupboards that hadn't been investigated for months or years.

Nothing was stolen or missing at all. Perhaps everything had been mislaid, put in the wrong place or simply ignored. Sales at Perkins were the best they had been for ages. What's more Davey was delighted and Monty kept his job. He could even afford to buy a new bicycle.

Food For The Dog

Tim, our dear black Labrador, preferred not to eat dog food that came in cans. He liked the food we ate and especially enjoyed Sunday when there were leftovers from the roasted joint for him to relish. My father used to buy very cheap cuts of meat and cook them for Tim. They were boiled for a while in an old saucepan that was reserved to cook meat for the dog and once or twice a week Tim's food was prepared. Our dear friend was hugely delighted and showed his appreciation by scoffing the food with amazing speed then looking with pleading eyes as he hoped for a second helping.

One summer we had a French boy staying with us for three weeks. He came to improve his language skills. When he arrived we soon realised that his English was extremely limited. Although we did our best to make him welcome Henri was clearly not very happy and for a whole week he didn't smile.

In the second week of Henri's stay we were due to have our family holiday. There was plenty of space in the Land Rover for the entire luggage, Tim, Henri, my brother, me and even my beloved teddy bear.

The night before we set off on our holiday my father prepared some meat for Tim then decided it was time for us to visit his parents at Chamford, as we wouldn't be seeing them for over two weeks. Henri came with us and remained silent, probably unable to understand much of what was said. He struggled with English at any time and so hearing my grandfather's rural accent must have been a trial for him. He sat unsmiling so my brother and I took him outside to play French cricket. We balked at the thought of explaining the English game to him.

Eventually we had to leave; it was time for me to go to bed as we would be making an early start. My brother and I, and even Henri, left my grandparents with silver coins given to us to spend on holiday. Grandpa was always very generous. We drove home along quiet lanes enjoying the evening sun that made the trees and glades glow in a special way. As we approached our house the Land Rover suddenly accelerated then came to an abrupt halt outside our home and my father leapt out and ran to the door. He had realised that the meat for Tim had been left simmering in the saucepan and we had been away for nearly three hours. Moments later the kitchen window was flung open and a blackened foul saucepan was projected with force into the garden. We stood open-mouthed and then we heard a quiet French chuckle. Henri, who had been stony-faced for a whole week, had at last smiled. Inspection of the mangled and twisted saucepan revealed the only thing left of Tim's meat was a charred piece of what might have been liver. It was the size of a shrunken chipolata.

'A blackened foul saucepan was projected with force into the garden…'

As we approached the kitchen foul acrid yellow smoke billowed through the open door. Somewhere inside was my father flapping a newspaper as he tried to clear the fug. The noisome odour had permeated the entire house and a yellow greasy film covered everything in the kitchen.

That night was warm and balmy which was a good thing as the stench was so strong we had to sleep with all of the windows wide open. Early the next morning we set off on our holiday. The sun shone, the beaches were sandy and every day was perfect. Saucepans and dog meat and foul yellow smoke were all forgotten. But after two weeks of summer bliss we had to return to The Forest and Henri was due to go back to France.

When we reached home our memories were soon revived. We opened the door of our home and the odours from two weeks before were still wafting around our home. The curtains needed washing, the surfaces cleaning and the windows had to be kept open for a week!

Bed And Breakfast

Mrs Stevenson ran The Old Forge Tea Rooms and also offered bed and breakfast accommodation for passing travellers. Her premises were very picturesque with a colourful garden that had many entertaining features; a wishing well, a fountain, a trickling stream and a pond that was well protected so that there was no risk of children falling in. This was not to safeguard any child but to protect Mrs Stevenson's finances in case she was sued as a result of an accident. She didn't really like children and never offered any assistance or a reduction in prices when children were about. A pale and weak glass of squash cost just as much as a cup of tea. If a visitor brought a baby and special food that needed heating, Mrs Stevenson would attend to the food willingly and charmingly but then add a few pence to the bill for service.

Outside The Old Forge was a smart 'Bed and Breakfast' sign and Mrs Stevenson made the most of the passing trade. She began with two cramped rooms into each of which beds were squeezed together with a small cabinet in between them. There was no wardrobe as there wasn't enough space. Instead there were hooks behind the door and a small towel rail was screwed to the wall. Nothing else could be fitted in to the rooms and two people could not move around at the same time.

People would see the sign and call in.

'I can accommodate you,' Mrs Stevenson would say.

'What do you charge?'

'Three pounds.'

'Very reasonable That's fine.'

'You'll pay me now.' This was plainly said and it was an order, not a request. The money would be handed over and then came the sting.

'I expect you'll want breakfast?'

'Of course.'

'That will be another two pounds each then, please.'

And the unsuspecting guests would calmly pay some more money realising that they had been tricked but unable to do anything about it. Payment made, the guests would be shown to their tiny room and many must have felt that they had been hoodwinked.

Almost all of Mrs Stevenson's trade came from people passing through The Forest and her business grew until she was turning customers away. She did not like doing this and so she decided to expand her premises. She was making enough money to have some more bedrooms but these were of an unusual nature. Mrs Stevenson bought a shed, erected it in her back garden, decorated and furnished the interior and began offering her additional accommodation. She felt a little uncertain about this venture but found that when The Forest was full of tourists they would gratefully accept what she had to offer. As there was an outside lavatory at the rear of her house there was no sanitation problem.

The shed was so successful that Mrs Stevenson bought some more and had them placed round the garden. Each rustic bedroom was individually decorated, not because Mrs Stevenson had an eye for design; she simply bought whatever fabric and paint were available cheaply. Each shed was given the name of a tree and her paying guests thought that this was a charming touch.

Each shed was given the name of a tree and her paying guests thought that this was a charming touch…

The Old Forge Tea Rooms were very popular with visitors to The Forest. As there was no rival for miles Mrs Stevenson attracted all the trade from parched passing day-trippers and holidaymakers and she took advantage of her supremacy. Guests willingly or unwillingly paid nearly twice as much for a pot of tea and some scones as they might in Humbury or even in Salchester. The delightful gardens were some compensation for the additional expense but not all guests were content with the prices. Not that this bothered the proprietress of the establishment. If anybody dared to comment on her prices they received a sharp reply.

'You are welcome to leave. You can try and find somewhere else.' Such visitors were all treated with equal charm and very few departed.

Occasionally there would be a complaint.

'These scones seem rather stale.'

'This cake is too dry.'

'This teacake is very chewy.'

Mrs Stevenson had a standard response. She would pull herself up to her maximum height, her bosom nearly bursting through her blouse, and bear down on the wayward customer who had dared to make a critical comment. Then in a very sharp tone she would say, 'I have been running these tea rooms for over twenty years and that is the first complaint that I have ever, ever received.' The errant victim would thus be cowed into submission and nothing more would be said.

At times Mrs Stevenson could mislead someone by appearing generous. A request for some hot water would be greeted with seemingly warm words.

'Of course you can have more hot water. There's plenty of it.' Little did the customer know that they would be paying for this privilege.

Mrs Stevenson always had her mind set on where she could make a few extra pennies for her business. Any unsuspecting person might fall foul of her cunning ways. As she required regular deliveries of bread and milk it would seem normal and reasonable to keep the delivery people good humoured but Mrs Stevenson did not think in a normal or reasonable manner. Everybody was a victim to be exploited.

A new baker was on his rounds. He was pleased his round included delivery to The Old Forge Tea Rooms as he had been told that Mrs Stevenson was a good customer. He didn't know anything else about her.

'Good morning, are you my new baker?'

'That's right, madam.'

'Well make sure you take care of me. I need bread and cakes and crumpets and buns every day you deliver.'

'Thank you, madam. Now what would you like today?'

'Four sliced white, two sliced brown and a dozen teacakes. Have you got all that?'

'Certainly, madam.'

The requested items were brought from the van and given to Mrs Stevenson who duly paid for everything and gave a warm and misleadingly friendly smile.

'Thank you, baker. That's excellent. Now would you like a cup of tea?'

'That would be very kind.'

'No trouble at all. Take a seat and I'll have it ready in a jiffy.'

The baker sat down at a table in the garden. He was glad of a pause in his deliveries. Mrs Stevenson soon appeared with a cup of tea.

'Here you are.'

'Thank you, just what I need.'

But the baker was about to be surprised. Pulling herself into her dominant stance Mrs Stevenson spoke.

'That will be nine pence, please.'

The Woman Bishop

The Diocese of Salchester stretches throughout The Forest and includes neighboring counties. Most of the churches are quaint, often tucked in quiet villages that have seldom seen much change. Few new homes are built and life goes on at a measured pace as if the days are just gently drifting along dreamily, leaving trees to mature and villages to remain steeped in history. Everything about the area is very traditional and little of note ever happens. Time ticks slowly especially in The Forest, Humbury and Salchester. When something newsworthy occurs everyone is totally surprised and occasionally even shocked.

'A woman!' exploded the Dean. 'A woman to be the next Bishop of Salchester!'

'If that's what the Archbishop of Canterbury has agreed to, then we have no choice,' said the Archdeacon.

'Well, the ABC is wrong! The cathedral and the congregation won't stand for it! Salchester is the most traditional diocese. A woman bishop would be unthinkable.'

'God will help us. If there is a problem God will make things right. He is always there, keeping a watchful eye.'

'Sometimes God needs guidance,' said the Dean with a contemptuous snort.

'Whatever do you mean?'

The Dean mulled things over. Outright opposition would be useless but subtle undermining…would that work? No, that would be too slow. Perhaps a sign from…God…yes…a sign from God. That was the answer. God might need some help in giving the sign of course; He couldn't be left to do all of His work on His own.

Amelia Rebecca Consuela Worthington–Matravers was enthroned as 57th Bishop of Salchester with due ceremony. The Dean could not have been more helpful to her; he could not have been more polite, more considerate or indeed self-effacing. Amelia soon regarded him as a loyal man whom she could trust and rely upon for wisdom and sensible advice. Little did she know that his well-mannered subservience was a carefully concocted part of the Dean's long-term strategy.

'Call me Milly,' Bishop Amelia said one day. 'What shall I call you?'

'Er…er…call me Dean.'

'So you're called Dean, Dean!' she said with a chuckle not recognising the put down that she had just received.

At the end of each day, when duties were done, dinner was complete and he had time to plan, the Dean retired to his study, a large glass of port in his hand, and sat in deep contemplation. This was not about ecclesiastical business, or theological problems, biblical matters or the past errors of his ways. He was thinking of how God should give His sign that this appointment was wrong and that He was displeased. The Dean had been a scientist and as the evenings drifted by he began to realise that his past could provide the answer. An explosion, a harmless but loud bang with some smoke…that could be a sign…but from where?…and how?…There must be no evidence after all.

It was as he officiated at a service with the woman that he privately referred to as 'the enemy' that the Dean began to formulate his master plan. There she was in front of him holding the bishop's special prayer book. Magnificently decorated and with an ornate clasp that held it tightly closed, this prayer book would be the source of God's divine dictum. The Dean was responsible for the care of the prayer book and by tradition he presented it to the Bishop whenever she officiated. Furthermore he also kept an identical copy locked away in his safe, in case of an accident or emergency.

Evenings of contemplation were replaced by sessions of experimentation. Clever plans were created and tested until at last the Dean achieved a solution. As the woman opened her prayer book the releasing of the clasp would trigger an electrical signal to a theatrical explosion from behind the altar. There would be a lightning flash followed by a bang and some smoke. God would have spoken and spoken clearly. It would be spectacular but not dangerous…yet…plainly significant. The Dean was not worried about discovery. A tiny battery and some wires could easily be inserted into the spine and covers of the prayer book. After the event he would be the first to investigate the cause and the equipment could quickly be hidden in his capacious robes. There would be no sign of any human involvement. Everything would be regarded as an Act of God. There would be no indication that God had been helped in expressing His opinion.

Having decided how God would be helped the Dean then had the problem of deciding when that help should be given. Obviously it must be at a very public occasion when many people would witness God's clear sign.

'When is the next major service?'

'Easter,' replied the Archdeacon.

'Even at Easter there's not a big enough congregation,' commented the Dean.

'Big enough for what?' asked the Archdeacon.

'I…I…just meant that our congregations are not what they were,' the Dean said hastily as he realized that his phraseology was not as subtle as it should have been.

'A month later the ABC is visiting,' the Archdeacon said casually.

'The ABC coming to Salchester! Why have I not been informed?' The Dean's face began to glow with fury.

'You have, you just don't check your emails regularly.'

'Oh…mmm…ah…'

'The ABC is giving his full support to the appointment of woman bishops,' added the Archdeacon. 'That's why he's coming to Salchester.'

The Dean was thrilled, as now he knew when God should speak.

The great day arrived and in a majestic procession the ABC strode into the cathedral together with the Bishop and all the church hierarchy of Salchester. The organ trumpeted, rumbled and groaned its way through successive hymns and the cathedral choir, mellifluous as ever, sung celebratory anthems. As the woman bishop stood to lead prayers the Dean handed her the prayer book and watched as she prepared to undo the clasp. She waited for silence then with the faintest click the book was opened. The click was followed by a tiny popping sound from behind the altar and some smoke slowly rose, formed a ring, hovered over the Bishop's head like a fluffy halo and then dispersed.

'A fluffy halo…'

The Archbishop stood open-mouthed. The congregation gasped. The Dean stood shocked and the Archdeacon, by his side, muttered, 'A sign. A sign from God! He moves in mysterious ways.'

'His wonders to perform,' mumbled the Dean.

Spirited Nights

You could not find a more traditional village in The Forest than Chamford. With its village green, historic cottages and active cricket club it seems to be the perfect place to live. There is even a rippling stream running through the village in which trout are easily spotted, as the water is so clear. Amongst the old buildings was The Brown Bear, a hostelry that dates from as far back as the thirteenth century although most of the building is more modern, having been built in Tudor times. This historic building is much admired and photographed by the many visitors to The Forest. Arthur Goodbody, the jovial landlord, made everybody welcome and he had a thriving business.

After living there for several years, and enjoying every day of his life, Arthur was suddenly perturbed. He was not as jolly as usual, his eyes lost their sparkle and he looked worried most of the time.

'Summat wrong, Arthur?' his regular customers would ask.

'No, nothing wrong, just not sleeping too well. Deirdre's the same. We just can't sleep.'

'That's not good. Yer need yer sleep. What's stopping yer sleeping?'

But Arthur wouldn't tell anyone about his problems, as he didn't want to be laughed at. Every night, after closing time, he and his wife, Deirdre, would tidy up, clean up, lock up and then retire to bed. They'd settle down to sleep and usually slumber until the next day. This had been their routine for years but things began to change. In the darkest part of a night they were woken by some loud bangs that seemingly came from down below. They were over in a few moments and then there was silence.

'What on earth was that?' asked Deirdre.

'A few stools must've toppled over. I can't have

stacked them properly.' But really Arthur knew that he had done his work well. He had just made the suggestion to calm his wife.

The next morning Arthur wondered if what he had said was true as when he went down to the bar several stools, that he had placed on the bar tables, were strewn over the floor. Puzzled, but beginning to feel rather silly, Arthur picked up the stools and then carried on with his day as if nothing had happened. He did notice that an old door, that lead to a storeroom, had been left ajar, so he shut it firmly.

For several nights there were no more disturbances but a week or so later Arthur and Deirdre were troubled again. This time some of the bangs were louder and the noises went on for longer. Deirdre woke and began to shake with fear. Arthur held her tight as the bangs and then some rumblings could be heard coming from down below.

'What is it? What is it?' Deirdre wailed.

'I don't know. But I'm going to sort it out.'

'You take care. It could be burglars.'

'I'll take care.'

Arthur went downstairs. In a stand he saw his father's strong ebony walking stick so he grabbed it and went to the bar and listened at the door. The noises seemed to have ceased but there was a sudden crash and then silence. Arthur thought for a moment. Should he go in? Should he stop and listen? He wasn't sure what would be best. Then he decided to only reach in and put on the lights. He opened the door just wide enough to slip his hand through and press the switch. He switched on the lights and pulled his hand back then shut the door. As he did so a shiver passed through him.

'Why's am I suddenly so cold?' he thought to himself.

There were no more noises so he threw the door open and stared in to the bar. Stools were over turned, a table was tipped on its side, part of a curtain was torn and the place looked as if a wild animal had been trapped and tried to escape. Totally puzzled Arthur decided to go back to Deirdre and what he regarded as the safety of being upstairs. As he left the scene he did notice that the same door had been left open. Without realizing what he had done Arthur left the lights switched on. There were no more disturbing noises that night.

For weeks the disturbances went on. Usually the bangs and crashes came on one or two nights a week. There might be a couple of weeks without disturbance and then life felt almost normal but as they settled each night Arthur and Deirdre prayed for a peaceful sleep. The noises always returned. If there had been a long spell without them then the bangs, crashes and even clangs would be heard for several nights in succession.

Poor Deirdre could take no more. She went to stay with a neighbour and refused to return until the problem was over. Arthur decided it was time for action. After closing time one evening he poured himself a large measure of rum, picked up the ebony walking stick, put out all the lights and settled in to a little alcove in the bar. The curtains were drawn back but a little light came through the old windows. Slowly Arthur sipped his rum. He enjoyed rum. He had been a sailor and he was planning to put his past ways to use.

Nothing happened for ages then suddenly Arthur sensed he was not alone. The temperature of the room seemed to drop. Arthur remained where he was but quietly swallowed what was left of his rum.

Crash! A stool toppled to the floor.

Bang! Another one followed.

Bang! Crash! Two more stools fell.

'Right!' boomed Arthur. 'I know you're here, whoever you are!'

A bang and a crash followed from different parts of the bar.

A bang and a crash followed…

'So there are two of you! Well, you don't frighten me! I can make loud noises too. Listen to this!'

Arthur thwacked the ebony stick down on the nearest table. It made a crisp and fearsome noise. 'Take that!' he bellowed. And then he thwacked the stick down again and again.

'I am not having you snivelling spirits ruining my life! Now listen to this!' he thwacked the stick down again. 'You are a load of…'

Arthur then let out a stream of insults peppered with every swear word an old sailor could think of. After every short shocking, foul filthy, indecent and improper word he banged his stick and then drew breath. There was silence but the air was still chilly.

'Have you got that into your stupid, thick…?' And then the obnoxious and offensive, terrifying torrent of profane words began again and the ebony stick was banged and banged.

Suddenly the air had lost its chill. Arthur no longer felt he had company and he returned to bed. A few weeks passed and the furniture stayed in place. Deirdre returned and all was well. Never again were they disturbed in the night but Arthur kept the ebony stick close at hand, just in case…

Take A Pair Of Sparkling Eyes

Humbury Operatic Society's annual production was in rehearsal and the cast was meeting three times weekly to prepare for performances of Gilbert and Sullivan's 'The Gondoliers'. Jeb Carpenter's artistic skills were well known as he could produce some very fine pictures reminiscent of John Constable. He always signed his pictures but somehow the name Jeb Carpenter looked similar to the signature of John Constable. This was partly because his names began with the same initial letters as the great artist. Because of the success of his atmospheric woodland scenery for 'Babes in the Wood' Jeb was asked if he could paint the Venetian set needed for the show. Always one to enjoy an artistic challenge he researched the works of Canaletto and to practise painted some pictures in his style. He reduced his signed name to 'Carpenter' but such was the vagueness of the letters that some people misread the signature. Set in historic frames Jeb's Canaletto style pictures were almost as popular as his scenes in the style of John Constable.

As opening night loomed Jeb was often working whilst soloists rehearsed and he soon picked up the tunes and the words of songs. He was very taken with the character of the Duke of Plaza-Toro and soon found himself softly singing the words as he created his Canaletto back scene with deft strokes of his brushes.

'In enterprise of martial kind,
When there was any fighting,
He led his regiment from behind—
He found it less exciting.
But when away his regiment ran,
His place was at the fore, O—
That celebrated,
Cultivated,
Underrated Nobleman,
The Duke of Plaza-Toro!'

But one night there was nobody to sing the role of the Duke.

'We need a replacement Duke,' the director explained to Jeb. 'He's broken his leg so he really can't perform.'

'Oh dear,' said Jeb, 'sarry to 'ear that.' He was secretly not displeased as he had enjoyed picking up the words as he painted. 'I could do it if you'm like…I mean if you carn't foind anyone else.'

'Could you really?'

'Carse I can.'

'You'll have to learn the dialogue as well.'

'That's naw problem,' declared Jeb, 'I knaw most of it already.'

News that Jeb was performing in 'The Gondoliers' soon spread to Whytteford and this resulted in the villagers organising an evening outing to see the show.

In Humbury's Assembly Rooms the orchestra stretched across the floor in front of the stage. As there was no orchestra pit the heads of the players obscured some of the view. Those sitting in more central seats spent the evening swaying heads to the left and right trying to look round the conductor who made excited flailing gesticulations as he tried to keep the musicians together.

All began well. The entire audience gasped with delight when the curtains opened to reveal Jeb's Canaletto style set. Ella Landy was surprised as she was used to having one of Jeb's pictures of Salchester Cathedral on her wall. Jeb's artistry was so reminiscent of Constable's style that one or two pictures had featured in sale rooms, unfortunately with the wrong attribution.

'Well I never,' she said, 'well I never.' And she couldn't take her eyes from the set.

The entire audience gasped with delight when the curtains opened to reveal Jeb's Canaletto style set…

Naturally the Duke of Plaza-Toro and his entourage arrive in Venice by means of a gondola. Ropes and pulleys were used and in all the tests the gondola had glided smoothly. After the dress rehearsal a little oiling should have been carried out as the loaded gondola had squeaked as it progressed across the stage. Somehow this had been forgotten and suddenly the squeaking was heard even above the sound from the orchestra. The gondola struggled on to the stage, the ropes hauled by two burly stagehands, but it wasn't moving very freely and they had never rehearsed with all of the characters on board. Consequently they nodded to each other and gave a mighty heave. With a shrill series of squeaks the gondola shot on to the stage and rapidly progressed to the opposite side until a hefty leg shot from the wings and blocked its path, bringing the vessel to an abrupt and juddering halt. The Duke and his family swayed precariously as they climbed from the gondola.

Unfortunately as they stepped from it the gondola began to return from whence it came as another member of the stage crew attempted to bring it back to the centre of the stage. The Duchess then gave a loud squeal that was repeated by the forty-two-year-old lady who was playing her teenage daughter.

Jeb had worked very hard learning his role and he looked magnificent in period costume. However although he knew all of the words certain aspects of the part defeated him. When sung with the rich accent of The Forest W. S. Gilbert's carefully constructed verses somehow had a fresh humour that was never intended.

'In enterproise of marrrtial koind,
When there warss any foighting,
He led his regimenn from behoind—
He farnd it less excoiting.
But when away his regimenn ran,
His place was aat the fore, O—
That celeebrated,
Culteevated,
Underrated Noblemaan,
The Dook arf Plaza-Tora!'

The show progressed and the chorus of gentlemen gondoliers did their best. Unfortunately some had been singing a chorus from 'The Mikado' whilst attempting to help each other into costumes in the dressing room. Suddenly realising they were due to appear the men arrived a little breathless at the side of the stage just in time for one of their entrances. They piled on stage with the ladies as the singing began.

'Dance a cachucha, fandango, bolero,
Xeres we'll drink—Manzanilla, Montero—
Wine, when it runs in abundance, enhances
The reckless delight of that wildest of dances!'

sang the ladies. But the men, forgetting they were in Venice burst out with;

'If you want to know who we are,
We are gentlemen of Japan:
On many a vase and jar—
On many a screen and fan...'

The conductor joined in singing the right words to the men and emphasising his lip movements. He was not one of the world's great conductors and multi-tasking was not in his repertoire. In consequence his animated beat became more eccentric. Like many conductors he could not sing in tune and his voluble off-key contribution was heard by most of the audience. Unfortunately a light shining at an awkward angle was hitting the chorus and their eyes were blinded so much that they couldn't really make out what their leader was trying to show them. Eventually order was restored and everybody was singing approximately in time.

The most famous aria in 'The Gondoliers' is 'Take a Pair of Sparkling Eyes'. The tenor singing the role of the gondolier, Marco, was about forty-seven years too old for the part. He still had the remains of a fine light tenor voice, and a selection of his notes was worth hearing but no amount of make-up or a well-chosen wig could disguise the fact that he was old enough to be the grandfather of the character that he was playing. Eventually his famous moment arrived and he began;

'Take a pair of sparkling eyes,
Hidden, ever and anon,
In a merciful eclipse—
Do not heed their mild surprise—
Having passed the Rubicon,
Take a pair of rosy lips.'

This tenor certainly thought that he could sing and he did his best to hit the correct notes. One of his problems was that he also had a lisp and so the beauty of the famous aria was lost as every 's' sound was sprayed from his lips. Being a man of some age he no longer had his own teeth. He was the owner of what had once been a fine set of dentures but as he had lost weight they no longer fitted his gums properly. After every few words he clenched his mouth firmly, trying to secure his set of teeth in his mouth.

The aria has a number of high notes that have to ring out to be effective. Naturally this requires the singer's mouth to be well open for the notes to be fine and clear and so he opened his jaw wide. As he did so the dentures sensed freedom and tried to escape. Consequently after each high note the singer's hand shot to his mouth to capture the wayward false teeth and restore them to their home. On his final high note he threw caution out with his voice and the dentures flew from his mouth and performed a neat arc to land upon the conductor's music stand. The orchestra finished playing and the audience began clapping. Their curiously enthusiastic applause did not hide an outburst of pent up laughter. There were cries of 'encore' and the tenor looked at the conductor with a hint of terror on his face. He was relieved to see that the conductor was not nodding his head.

Village School

My grandfather and old Harry attended the Whytteford village school at the same time. Harry was a little older than Grandpa but that was of no consequence as they quickly became friends.

'Ah, we 'ad 'appy toimes,' drawled Harry, 'but there waz one diff'rence between us.'

'What was that?' I asked.

'We…e…e…ll,' drawled old Harry, 'let's put it this way. Yer granfer waz the best behav'd boy in the class and Oi was the worsen.'

'Were you really?'

'Oi didn' loike school. Once Oi could read'n write a bit Oi soon got bored so although Oi went to school each mornin' Oi escaped soon as Oi could.'

'Was it so bad?' I asked.

'Lookin' back Oi s'pose it wasn't. We learnt our writing and our sums using slates and slate pencils.'

'We use books today.'

'I knaw yer do. But we managed on our slates. Yer granfer had noice neat writing an' he was good at his sums too. That was'im not me. I wanted adventures.'

'How did you have adventures?'

'We…e…e…ll, we 'ad just one teacher, Mr Boomer, who had a voice to suit 'is name. Gaw, he couldn' 'arf bellow. When you wuz in trouble yer didn' 'arf knaw it!'

'Was that frightening?'

'Yer soon gart used to 'him. Actually he waz a koind man and'e took care of us real well. There waz abart forty of us in the class, mixed ages moind, and he taught us all. There waz kids as young as foive and up to fourteen. We didn' sit at desks, there waz a great roise of seats that got higher, young'uns at the front and older'uns hoigh up at the back. That way old Boomer could keep 'iz eyes on us all, but he didn' have eyes in the back of his head! That's 'ow Oi used to escape from the classroom. When'e was busy at the blackboard writing with chalk he couldn' see what us lot waz up to.'

Harry's story was fascinating. His school was so different from the one that I attended. I had only seen rising seats in photographs and cartoons but Harry and my grandfather had used them every day that they went to school. It was those rising seats that provided the means for his escape and his adventures.

'Oi always used to sit up at the baack,' drawled Harry. 'Close by the windor. On sunny dayz The Forest was callin' me. Oi wanted to be out'n abart, over the common and into the woods. When ole Boomer's eyes waz turned away from uz Oi'd slip out through the windor an run as farst as Oi could away from the school an' into the open air.'

My grandfather and old Harry attended the village school at Whytteford at the same time…

'But what did you do?'

'Arrrrrgh! What didn' Oi do? Oi wasn' the only one to escape from Boomer. Three or faw've us would hop through the windor an arf to the open air. We'd go round behind the cattages close boi the school an'then slip over the road and up to the race course.'

'The race course,' I asked. 'Where is the race course?'

'We…e…e…ll, if yer go up past The Cobblers you'm see a smooth, broad graassy strip 'tween two hedges. That's the race course. There 'aven't been proper races there for years'n years now but there used to be. Charabancs used to come out from Salchester to Whytteford Races an' the railway even ran special trains when Oi was young.'

Harry was telling me about the history of Whytteford revealing past events that few other villagers could remember. He would suddenly recount tales of times past, slipping them into conversation as if everybody already knew them.

'When we gart there we'd chase the donkeys up the race course. Then we'd stop the chase and they'd calm down and start munching at the gorse bushes. The gorse was grown up where the turf used to be all smooth'n green. We'd creep rarnd the bushes and jump on the donkeys and start racing them. Gaw! That were great fun. We'd race'm up an down the course, falling off and jumpin' back on again! We waz young and loively and it seemed easy. 'Twas more fun than listening to old Boomer anyway!'

'Did Boomer ever notice you were missing?'

'Funny yer should arsk that. He knew some of uz was missing but he waz never sure who! We didn' do it every day; only when the weather was lovely in the summer.'

'What did you do when the weather wasn't so good?'

'If it'was rainin' we'd stay indoors and try and learn what Boomer was teaching. But if there was a cold spell and the ponds and lakes were frozen we'd escape the same way, but shut the window behind us. We didn' want our mates to get cold.'

'So what happened then?'

'We'd be arf over the common to Standmoor Pool.

That'd be frozen over so we'd soon be skating or playing a game. There waz so few of us and so we swept over the lake on the skates so fast we could 'ardly see each ozzer. Ah! Gran' toimes. Gran' toimes.'

'What else happened?'

'Naw, lets 'ave a think'um.'

There was a short pause as Harry's mind drifted back in time. We were sitting in a sunny spot in his garden. It was summer and the bees were gathering nectar from lavender and honeysuckle.

'Ah,' he suddenly said. 'T'was on a lovely day loike this'un. Three ov us was fed up wi' bein' in the classroom an' for once yer granfer was one ov us'n. We slipped out through the window an' we waz off'naway to Standmoor Pool. Gaw, it was hot and the water looked so cool an' temptin' we decoided to 'ave a swim. We didn' ave no costumes so we jus' swam. Nobody was abart so we didn' care. We moight 'ave cared if us'd known what would happen next. Yer see…'

Suddenly Harry stopped.

'You'm better arsk yer granfer abart what happened,' he said. 'Tis more 'is story than moine an'e may nart want you to know abart it!'

The Gorse Was In Bloom…

Eventually my grandfather started talking about Standmoor Pool. I didn't like to ask him leading questions and so I was delighted when he gradually began to talk about this quiet and secluded spot.

'Have you taken that young beauty of yours to Standmoor Pool. 'T'is a foine spot for sunbathing in a noice little bikini.' Grandpa always had an eye for a pretty girl and he took an active interest in my affairs with young ladies. How did he know that Mandy had a bikini? Perhaps having seen her Grandpa had used his imagination. I decided not to ask any questions.

'The garse never storps bloomin' at Standmoor.' There was a cheeky twinkle in his eye. 'A nice spot to take yer girl and know you won't be seen…' he added mischievously. 'Though we was,' he muttered in an undertone.

'What ever do you mean?' I asked.

'T'was on 'n'ot day in the summer. School would soon be over for a week or so but 'ol Harry n'I 'ad 'ad enough.'

This was becoming interesting!

'We decided there was no point us bein' cooped up. We'm wanted freedom. So we'm decided to escape when ole Boomer wasn' looking.'

I was amazed to hear this from my grandfather as old Harry had told me that he was the worst behaved boy in the school and my grandfather was the best behaved.

'We clambered owt'away before Boomer could see whart was 'appening. There was me, Harry and Josie.'

'Josie, isn't that a girl's name?'

'Naw,' said Grandpa. 'Tis short for Josiah. Anyways, t'was hot weather an' we went to Standmoor Pool. The warter looked clear an t'was so blue.'

'It always looks so blue on sunny days,' I said, trying to nudge Grandpa along.

'We'm undressed and splashed abart in the pool. It's

not thart deep but the warter was cool and refreshin'. We could swim a bit so we cooled ar'selves and then stretched out on the turf to dry.'

Grandpa's story was becoming most intriguing. I had to force myself to think of him as an active youth and not as an old man who grew vegetables and kept chicken.

'Arfter a whoile we was dry so we thought we'd better be put'n clothes on. T'was then we saw they weren't where we'd left'em.'

'What had happened? Had someone hidden them?'

'Oh no. But they'm warn't where we'd left'em, either. We looked about an'there was the clothes draped over the garse bushes in full view!'

'Who had done that?'

'That's what we'm wonder'd. We couldn't see a soul, but then we'eard some giggling from behoind some bushes. Girly giggling, t'was.'

'What did you do?'

'What could us do? We had to get our clothes so we dashed acrarse the grass, grabbed the clothes and slipped'em on farst as us could. All the toime we'm could hear this girly giggling. Soon as us was orl dressed we went to where the giggling was but they'm orl gone.'

'Really? They must have been quick.'

'Oi reckon they'm not garn far. Probably hoiding in some other bushes. We'm made our ways home arter that.'

'Was that all that happened?'

'Naw.' Grandpa paused for a moment. 'Oi guess oi can tell you now. Arter all you'm be having yer own fun.'

'Tell me what.'

'Few day later school had finished for the summer. Oi was in Humbury an one of the girls from school saw me. "Enjoy your swim?" she says. There was a sparkling cheeky look in her eyes'n all.'

'What did you say?'

'I asked what she was talking abart. But I knew what she meant and I loiked that look in'er eyes. So I asked her to come walkin' with me. Next day we went walking and we went to Woodbine Wood. Tis quiet there and well away from prying eyes. We used to go there a lot.'

'Did you take her for many walks?' I asked.

'Aye,' said Grandpa. 'And we'm still walking together! We married a few years later on 21st December. The garse was in full bloom and has been ever since for us.'

'The gorse was in full bloom and has been ever since for us.'

Suddenly Grandpa's eyes, already gleaming, sparkled in delight.

'Can you guess what people said at our wedding?' he asked.

'Something about the gorse?'

'N…a…w.' He dragged out that word as he mused for a moment. 'They'm said we gart married that date 'cos it's the shortest day, but it's also the longest noight!'

The Cuckoo Comes In April…

'The cuckoo will soon be here,' said my grandfather.

'That's because it's April. You know the rhyme says, "The cuckoo comes in April…" so of course it will soon be here.'

'Ah, but there's more to it than thaat,' he said mysteriously. 'There's thirty days in April so the rhoyme doesn't tell you'm very much, now dussit?'

'What else is there to tell?' I asked.

'We…e…ll,' said Grandpa, stretching the word so that it seemed as if some great secret was about to be revealed. 'That rhoyme dussn't tell which day the cuckoo's comin', yer see.'

'How are we meant to know which day the cuckoo will arrive? It has to fly a long way.'

'Maybe he does fly a lo…ng way but he knows where he's going so he arrives on a particular day in that place.'

'Really? The cuckoo arrives on a particular date? Does it have a calendar?'

Grandpa chuckled. 'Course nart. He just knows! Now what's the date today?'

'It's April 10th.'

'Then he'll be in Whytteford in three days toime. The cuckoo always comes to Whytteford on April 13th, and he's never late.'

'Are you sure? Has the cuckoo never been a day late or a day early?'

'Never,' said Grandpa. 'I was born in Whytteford and all the years I lived there the cuckoo came on that day.'

I was rather dubious. Seasons vary. Surely the cuckoo must be late sometimes, especially if the spring was cold? Why should cuckoos leave warm places to fly to a country that is cool?

On April 12th that year a cold wind swept through The Forest shaking the trees but also blowing the clouds away leaving the sky clear and bright. Tim trotted after my father on his late walk but they soon returned. The cold wind had made my father red cheeked and the dog had suddenly started to run home. The air chilled rapidly, the temperature dropped and next morning we awoke to find the catkins on the birch trees decorated by a thick frost. Surely the cuckoo would stay away from Whytteford for a few more days?

No cuckoo calls could be heard from the woods. The trees were not silent as woodpeckers were busy giving their laughing calls. In The Forest the green woodpecker is called a yaffle, and when you hear it you realise that this is a perfect nickname. For once my grandfather was surely wrong. But by late afternoon the trees basked in warm sunshine, the sharp wind had dropped and the end of the day became balmy but no cuckoo calls were heard. The yaffles seemed to be enjoying themselves, perhaps they were laughing at the cuckoos.

The sun would soon be setting in the clear spring sky. From the woodlands a clear, crisp call cut through the air with a note of defiance. 'Cuckoo! Cuckoo! Cuckoo! Cuckoo!' Grandpa was right after all.

'Cuckoo! Cuckoo! Cuckoo! Cuckoo!'

And Sings All Day In May...

Mandy was staying with us for a weekend towards the end of May. Warm days had come to The Forest and as soon as I saw her tight-fitting blouse and short skirt a thrill ran through me. Close warm kisses did not calm either of us. Eventually it was time for bed and we had a final embrace in the kitchen. We thought that everybody had gone upstairs and so the kiss was prolonged.

'I wish you could be with me. Can't you creep in?'

'I can't,' I whispered longing to do as she asked and beginning another long kiss.

'Take me for a walk tomorrow.'

'We'll go to Woodbine Woods.'

Suddenly my mother swept into the kitchen.

'Hullo, Mum,' I said. 'What are you doing here?'

'Don't be silly.'

The door had been open. Had she heard anything?

'Good night. Off to bed now.' This was a command and there could be no discussion.

We parted and the incident was over.

We walked across the open common enjoying warm sun. We passed the tumulus and headed to the wood that was so often favoured by young lovers. My Great-Aunt Mabel certainly had happy memories of this quiet spot and some men of her age had pleasing recollections of Great-Aunt Mabel.

Occasionally we'd stop for a brief kiss then we looked towards the woodlands. Mandy's summer blouse, several buttons undone, gave thrilling glimpses of pleasures to come and her eyes shone with delight. Urgency delayed any more kissing until we reached the quiet woods where sweet-scented woodbine bloomed. We settled in a quiet spot and embraced passionately, bodies entwined and with testosterone on full charge time became irrelevant. It seemed there was nothing that could disturb young lovers.

There was a fluttering in the birch trees.

'Cuckoo! Cuckoo! Cuckoo! Cuckoo!'

The call was loud and clear.

'Cuckoo! Cuckoo!'

We couldn't ignore it.

'Cuckoo! Cuckoo!'

Would it never stop?

'Cuckoo! Cuckoo!'

Eventually we realised how long we had been enjoying the woodlands. Had Mabel been loved in the same spot? As we left the woods we heard that call again.

'Cuckoo! Cuckoo!'

And then the yaffle laughed from a nearby tree.

Were they laughing at us?

We made our way home past ponies, donkeys, stunted trees and heather spreading a haze of purple over the landscape. Here and there we saw clumps of gorse bushes with blooms of bright yellow flowers. I thought of my grandfather's words and whispered, 'When the gorse is in bloom loving's in fashion.'

And then the yaffle laughed from a nearby tree.

Election Time

A general election could cause a few ripples of excitement in The Forest but they seldom lasted for very long. The sitting candidate was Sir Arthur Winsom-Wilde and he was certain of a safe majority. His devotion to The Forest ensured continued support and his share of the poll barely fluctuated, often defying national trends. Sir Arthur lived and breathed the life of The Forest. He always had time for his constituents and never seemed to mind having a discussion on the High Street in Humbury or anywhere else.

Old Harry assured me that modern elections were boring compared with when he was young. As well as dropping stink bombs in The Cobblers Arms Harry and his pals indulged in other excitements. When Harry and my grandparents had been young the Liberal party was still a strong force. My grandfather always voted Liberal and even took the News Chronicle. When that paper closed down he never bought a national newspaper again.

'Best of all,' Harry said in his thick drawl, 'was the foires!'

'Fires? What had fires to do with elections?'

'Ah, young'n, youm'd be suppised!'

'I really don't understand.'

'Think abart it. When could the farm workers and the carters vote?'

'At the end of the working day, I suppose.'

'That's right. Now you'm might get the idea.'

'Go on, what happened.'

'This was before Sir Arthur's toime, yersee, when there was just Liberals and the other lart. The sitting candidate only had a toiny majaritty by the standards of The Forest and so we had to do our best for him. There waz a lot of radicals moved in at the time and if they all got to vote then their chappie moight have won. He wasn't even from The Forest and we wasn't 'aving 'im as our member of parl-ia-ment. So we had to do something. We couldn' fix the vote, t'would be illegal. But we could stop them from voting.'

'But how?'

'With a foire!'

'A fire! How did a fire change things?'

'Now then young'n use your magination,' he drawled. 'Just as they radicals waz gettin' home we started a fire on the common near where they waz living. The only thing that was damaged was a few old gorse bushes. The fire blazed away and out them radicals came and used beaters to put the foire out. If it looked loike they waz winning then somehow another foire began in some more bushes. Eventually the foires were all safely put out but by then the polls had closed and they radicals were done for.'

'Done for?'

'Yes, young'n they waz done for b'cos they couldn't vote!'

'How cunning! That was really clever,' I said.

'Oi don't supparse it made much difference, but my gawd it weren' 'alf fun.' Old Harry had a wicked look in his eyes. 'You arght to ginger up this here election,' he said. 'Put some fun into it!'

Ella Landy also had a tale to tell. She had lived for many years in a snug wattle and daub cottage with her husband. He used to deliver fruit and vegetables to the villages driving a smart green cart pulled by a chestnut horse. Ella worked for Lady Dusbury at Challington Manor and usually her dealings with her ladyship were amicable but every now and then there would be a little disagreement.

Polling day happened to fall on Ella's day off and so that morning she had put on a pinafore and was at home cleaning pots and pans in her kitchen. There was a steady drizzle outside so she had decided to vote later on in the day. Suddenly there was knock on the cottage door. Ella was rather surprised, as she wasn't expecting a visitor. She was even more surprised when she opened the door. There stood Lady Dusbury and not far away was an elderly Rolls-Royce with the chauffeur standing beside it.

'Ah, Ella,' said her ladyship, 'have you been to vote yet?'

'No, not yet. I have a few chores to finish.'

'Never mind them. The weather's miserable so you can come with me in the car.'

'But I'm not ready.'

'That doesn't matter. Come along.'

There was no point in arguing and so Ella, still wearing her pinafore, walked to the car with Lady Dusbury and climbed in after her. The chauffeur closed the door and gave Ella a cheeky smile. On the way the two passengers chatted easily with each other although Ella did feel embarrassed about what she was wearing.

When they reached the polling station Lady Dusbury took Ella to the notice board that listed the various candidates and pointed firmly at one of the names.

'That's the person you should vote for,' her ladyship declared. 'Make sure you do as I say.' Then she strode into the building and Ella followed in her billowing wake. The voting took just a few minutes, as there was scarcely a queue. In fact more time was spent discussing the weather and how the nights were drawing in. Then Lady Dusbury swept out with Ella close behind. They returned to the Rolls-Royce and the journey began.

'Did you vote for the person I told you to?' asked her ladyship.

Ella remained silent for a moment.

'Well, did you?'

'It's a secret ballot,' Ella replied.

If she was cross about something, Lady Dusbury had a tendency to sniff loudly. She didn't realise that she did this but Ella Landy was very aware of her ladyship's little habit.

Suddenly there was a loud sniff. They drove on and the sniffs continued.

'As a matter of fact,' said Ella, 'I voted for someone else.' As in those days few people stood for election that was a very clear statement.

The short journey suddenly seemed to take a long time as neither Ella nor Lady Dusbury spoke again. There was a crisp sniff every few seconds as her ladyship became increasingly irritated. When the car approached the end of the lane where Ella lived Lady Dusbury suddenly reached for the speaking tube.

'Stop the car at the end of the lane,' she snapped before giving a very loud sniff. 'Ella will walk the rest of the way.'

The Rolls-Royce came to a gentle halt and the chauffeur began to get out to open the door for Ella.

'No need for that,' snapped her ladyship. 'Ella can manage perfectly well on her own.'

The short journey suddenly seemed to take a long time…

The chauffeur remained in his seat and Ella opened the door.

'Thank you, madam,' she said once she was out of the car. 'Usual time in the morning?' she added with a cheeky smile.

It was a rhetorical question. Lady Dusbury stared straight ahead. Ella closed the door and the Rolls-Royce purred gently as it went on its way.

On one Election Day the weather was murky and a steady drizzle was falling. My mother tended to feel the cold and damp weather always made her extremely wary.

'Come on,' called my father, 'it's time we voted.'

Mother grabbed a coat to keep the damp out and the warmth in. They went to the village school, which for one day became the local polling station. Tellers, representing each of the candidates, were standing outside.

'Well, here's one that's definitely voting for us,' said one of the tellers.

My mother realised that she was wearing a bright coat in the colour of one of the major parties, but not of the one that she was supporting. From then on she always took care to wear neutral shades whenever there was an election until the day that turned out to be her final voting opportunity. Nearly ninety years old, but still very aware of her actions, she wore a rainbow striped cardigan that somehow included the colours of several political parties.

That must have either given hope to all of the tellers or confused them totally.

It's Just Plain Wrong

Icicles were hanging from the thatch of Jeb Carpenter's cottage and fingers of frost made patterns on the inside and outside of the windows.

'That fire's burning frosty tonight,' he muttered. 'Time to stay at home.' Cold clear nights always made fires burn with special brightness and that night was bitter. From all the cottages of Whytteford smoke drifted on the cold night air.

Jeb had plenty to do on winter nights. He sat close to the fire wielding paintbrushes and mixing colours carefully. As he worked his magic the shape of Salchester Cathedral appeared on the canvas. Jeb took his time, picked up a fine brush and added delicate details. Eventually he was content and he stopped work. 'Need to keep the cold out,' he said as he poured a good measure of whisky.

Icicles were hanging from the thatch of Jeb Carpenter's cottage

That winter the cruel coldness bit into the depths of The Forest. Trees split, the deer struggled to find soft moss to eat and the waters of the River Coble froze over. Jeb ventured out to buy food but most of the time he worked at his pictures. He could produce very fine pictures in the style of John Constable; always signed 'Jeb Carpenter' although the signature was not very clear and his initials were convenient.

Spring daffodils brought cheer to cottage gardens and cherry blossom bloomed. The bitter winter was at last over and tourists flocked to The Forest. At weekends Jeb hung his pictures on his garden fence. He dug the rich soil turning over the earth then he pulled a rake through the loam, smoothing it ready for seeds. At the same time he kept an eye on the pictures and listened.

'I do like the one of the cathedral.'

Jeb smiled to himself. Before long he would have some money in his pocket.

'It's very good. I wonder how much it is.'

Jeb continued pulling the rake through the soil but gradually moved closer to the pictures.

'Do you know anything about these pictures?'

'I should do 'cos t'was me that painted them.'

A few minutes later the picture was sold and Jeb had a contented smile as well as money in his pocket.

Cuckoos called in the woods, the blossom of May-trees ushered in summer and the holidaymakers spread through The Forest. Jeb tied up his beans, sprayed the roses in his garden and sold his pictures. His winter work was very profitable.

When the cricket season was over Jeb looked at his shabby jacket and realised that he'd better buy some new clothes. He'd been invited to his niece's wedding. Bradbury and Littler were the best gentlemen's outfitters in the county so Jeb ventured to Salchester.

His business done Jeb left the outfitters smiling happily. He would look really smart at the wedding and his niece would be proud of him. He glanced across the street. 'That's a new shop over there, very smart too.' And then something caught his eye. He crossed the street and stared at the window. Why was one of his pictures for sale in a gallery in Salchester? It was his picture but it had been put in to an antique fancy frame.

The shop doorbell jangled as Jeb's bulky figure entered the gallery.

'Good morning, sir.'

Jeb cast his eye over the smooth young man in his slick suit.

'Ah…good marnin.'

'Have you come to view anything special?'

'Ah…that picture of er…Salchester Cathedral.'

'Very fine, we're very lucky to have it.'

'Ah…who'zit by?'

'John Constable.'

'Ah, izzit now?'

'Yes, sir. It's only just come on to the market.'

'Let me 'ave a look at 'im then.'

'Certainly, sir.' The assistant raised his eyebrow in disbelief but took the picture from the window.

Jeb eyes drifted carefully over the work of art.

'That ain't by Constable.'

'I assure you that it's been verified by experts at one of the country's leading galleries. We're privileged to have it here for a month.'

'Verified you say. Well, let me tell you this. It's just plain wrong!'

'Wrong, sir? What do you mean wrong? Look at the signature.'

'John Constable did not paint that picture and he didn't sign it.'

'But it's been verified as a newly discovered work from his time at Salchester. There is no doubt about it.'

'We…ll,' said Jeb, 'if that's what you say, I ain't ganner argue with'ee. But I tell you here'n now, that picture is wrong.'

'Can I ask why you are so certain of this, sir?'

'Ah,' said Jeb, 'you'm can ask but I ain't telling 'ee; but I'll tell 'ee this—'

'What's that, sir?'

'You'm better look abart for some more pictures by 'im. That's what I can tell 'ee!'

Jeb chuckled to himself. Autumn was in the air and in a few weeks time it would be winter when there would be long, dark, frosty nights.

Grandpa's Funeral

As I left for school one morning at the beginning of May the sun was shining warmly but there had been a harsh frost. The newly bright flowers on the azaleas in our garden were smothered with fine ice crystals. In a curious way death was in the air even though the morning was so bright. That afternoon, at two-thirty, I was looking at a picture that showed the funeral of Franz Joseph, the Emperor of Austria. Seek black horses with black plumes pulled the great hearse through the crowded streets of Vienna. This was a memorable scene. School finished and I returned home. My mother was waiting for me. 'There is some news,' she said, 'Grandpa died at half past two this afternoon.'

When I was a child death was barely discussed. An elderly friend had given me a book when I was six years old. Her name was Elizabeth and she had written a message inside the cover together with her name. 'Now you will remember me,' she said as she gave the book to me. A few weeks later I was told, 'We won't see Elizabeth anymore.' The word death was not mentioned. Other ancient friends and elderly relations 'passed away' or 'fell asleep'. Some 'passed on'; others I was told had 'gone to a better place' but nobody had died. I suppose my parents and grandparents must have attended funerals but in my presence no reference was ever made to these events. This was an age when such things were not spoken of in front of children. Now that I was almost an adult I was suddenly confronted with the fact that my grandfather really was dead.

About ten days later it was the day of his funeral in the church at Chamford. I dressed in a crisp white shirt.

'Put this on,' said my father as he thrust a black tie in my hand.

I put on my suit and before we left I was given a glass of sherry. We were all rather quiet as we drove to the village where my grandparents had lived for many years and arrived at the church. There was quite a gathering of people most of whom I did not know. Relations who we had not seen for many years had suddenly emerged from their houses and cottages. It struck me then how odd it is that people go to the funeral of someone who is dead that they had not bothered to visit for years when the person was alive. Are they trying to make up for past negligence? We processed into the church and as 'family' we sat in a pew in front of everyone else. The organist wandered his fingers over the keys producing a nondescript semi-dirge instead of some proper music. He suddenly brought his meanderings to a conclusion as the vicar announced a hymn.

As the hymn was sung the coffin containing my grandfather's body was brought in. Two high trestles had been placed in the aisle and when the coffin bearers approached them they raised their shoulders a little higher in preparation for lowering it upon the stands.

Two high trestles had been placed in the aisle…

Until this moment I had found the occasion sombre. I was saddened by the death of my kindly grandfather and prior to this I had never attended a funeral. The bearers stopped their slow procession next to the high trestles and gently lowered their burden. Unfortunately they had misjudged the positioning and as they moved away one end of the coffin began to rise. Grandpa was in danger of being vertical when he should have been horizontal. The bearers, realising their error, hastily put their shoulders beneath the coffin and heaved it forward before lowering it again, this time in a safe position. Grandpa would not be disturbed during his service.

Grandpa was in danger of being vertical…

The hymn came to its conclusion and the vicar stood up. He was a local man and spoke with the accent of the people of The Forest.

'Naw,' he said, 'I want you to turn to page fifty-six.' As he spoke he opened his service book. 'Naw, page fifty-eight.' He turned some pages. 'Naw it's not fifty-eight, 'tis fifty-six arter all.'

The service proceeded with disappointing calm after that exciting beginning. Tributes were made, prayers said and the final hymn was sung during which the bearers returned. This time they positioned themselves more carefully as they loaded the coffin on to their shoulders. I had not seen their progress as they entered the church at the beginning of the service but I studied their departure. No wonder there had been a problem when they arrived. Two of the bearers were six inches shorter that their colleagues and so grandpa's arrival and departure had been at an unusual and awkward angle.

There was an outburst of friendly chatting once the service was over and the congregation seemed almost cheerful as everybody left the church. Grandpa's funeral taught me that even on sad occasions there is sometimes a little humour to lighten the tone.

My grandfather had always taken a keen interest in his family. He would walk up the gravel track to our home and survey the scene, pausing to see how plants were growing and if the apple trees were bearing fruit. When visiting us he would sometimes decide to take a walk and meet me as I returned from school. This was always a delight as it meant that we would have some time together with nobody else listening.

'I expect you need some pocket money,' was a favourite sentence and some coins, worth quite a lot of chocolate, would be given to me.

A month passed. Grandpa was no longer with us but he was not forgotten. On a bright afternoon I looked out from our home and saw a familiar figure walking along. Was this my grandfather? The figure gently walked on surveying the scene in a familiar way, took a few steps and paused. He nodded his head as if he was assuring himself, 'They're all right. Yes, they are all right.' And then he moved. He had chosen a route that took him behind a big tree. I stood and watched but all I saw was the tree; just a tree. There was no sign of my grandfather.

The Gandyman

'It's time you learnt to drive,' said my father.

This was quite a surprise as driving had never crossed my mind. I was used to catching a bus to Humbury or Salchester. If I wanted to travel further I would use the trains and my father would always collect me from the station if I returned late in the day.

'It will save us collecting you and you will be able to do some deliveries for me as well.'

I could see his point and realised that I would gain independence and new freedom. A car would be also very useful when courting. I thought about the numerous quiet places where a car would be well hidden from prying eyes and decided that having a car had many possibilities. I remembered an evening when I had walked through The Forest to Broomhill and returned by quiet paths. Passing silently through one secluded spot I had seen a car, with windows steamed up, rocking gently as lovers entwined. This slightly erotic memory hastened my decision.

'I'm going to have driving lessons,' I said to Mandy, my delightful chestnut-haired girlfriend.

'That sounds good,' she replied. 'We'll be able to go almost anywhere in The Forest.' There was an almost salacious look in her eyes. 'You must know lots of quiet places.'

At first I practised on the long drive to our home; learning how to control a vehicle and manoeuvre it and avoid obstacles.

'Now for a three-point turn,' said my father once I had mastered basic moves.

At first I found it quite difficult.

'Pull forward to there.'

I found the right gear and the car crawled forward.'

'Stop. Now gently reverse but don't hit the shed.'

Ever so slowly I reversed the car.

'Stop.'

I stopped and had managed to avoid the shed.

'Now pull forward and turn to the right.'

We moved smoothly and my father looked pleased.

'Well done; carry on, you can manage on your own now.' He calmly opened the door and left me to practise.

After a few days of gently driving on a private gravel road I had mastered quite a lot of driving skills. My three-point turns were calmly accomplished and I could even manage to reverse quite a distance without slipping on to the grass.

Old Harry watched me as he trimmed some bushes.

'What you'm need is gandy-man,' he declared.

'A gandy-man? I've not heard of such a thing.'

'Oi could make you'm one but perhaps t'would be bessun not to 'ave'im.'

'But what is gandy-man?'

'We…e…ll.' Harry lifted a fork from his wheelbarrow and drove it into the soil then lent on it. 'I s'pose it 'appened round the toime you waz born. Jemmy Midgely wanted to learn 'ow to droive. Now don't you'm go tellin' folk but God din't give Jemmy much in the way've brains. He could droive quite well but 'e would never've passed the droivin' test. So 'e made 'isself a gandy-man to keep 'im company!'

'So 'e made 'isself a gandy-man to keep 'im company!'

I was beginning to realise what Old Harry was suggesting.

'T'was a good'n too. Jemmy made the figure jus' the roight soize an' sat'im in the car next to'im. He even dressed 'im up proper. Changed 'is clothes 'cording to the season an' all. He gave'im a name. Called'im Bertie. With his gandy-man Jemmy drove all over The Forest. He buzzed along the lanes 'n visited all the pubs and friends an' all, with Bertie keeping an eye on'm so to speak.'

'Did the police ever stop him?'

'Naw. They never saw'im. 'Ow often do yer see a pollisman rarnd this way? In them days they only 'ad boikes. Jemmy knew he wasn' likely to be found owt.'

'Did he do it for long?'

'Ah yes. Oi reckon he did it for fifteen years but then 'e'ad to starp.'

'Why? What happened?'

'Jemmy got a bit too venturous. He drove all the way to Humbury one night. Nothin' wrong with that. Pollissman in Humbury aren't very clever oither. Trouble waz Jemmy had a bit too much to drink that noight an' fell asleep in the Dusbury Arms. They knew'im there so they let'im sleep till next day. Trouble waz when Jemmy woke up he went back to'is car an Bertie was missing.'

'Missing? Hadn't he locked the car?'

'He'd turned the key in the lock but he'd turned it back again. So there was Jemmy with'is car but he could'n droive it as Bertie wasn' there. There waz the L plates on'm an all.'

'Did he find Bertie?'

'Naw. Jemmy niver drove again. He missed Bertie so much that he gave up droivin'. Probably best thing too. Roads gart busier and pollissman soon'ad some cars.'

I really didn't know what to make of Harry's tale. Would anyone be so bold as to drive around The Forest with a dummy for company?

'T'was a long toime ago,' said Harry, as if he was reading my thoughts. He gave a throaty chuckle. 'T'is a good tale, anyroads,' he added with a wicked glint in his eye.

Rural Remedies

Living in an historic area like The Forest one often encountered cures and customs that had faded away in places where modern medicines have become fashionable. Herbal remedies are still immensely popular, even today.

If you have a toothache, chew on some mint or have a cup of mint tea. If the toothache is very bad do both. Suffering from constipation? Then gather some dandelion leaves, chop and dry them then put a couple of teaspoons of the dried leaves in a mug and pour on some boiling water. Let the leaves steep for about ten minutes and drink the liquid. Do this three times a day and your constipation will soon pass.

These rural remedies are not appetising but can be effective. Or are they? Is it the thought of the cure that brings relief or the supposed benefit that the preparation offers? Often the medicine can seem worse than the ailment and so recovery is hastened. Certainly some treatments have doubtful benefits.

If you are suffering from acne, there are various cures that you might not want to try. Cover your spots with smooth clay. Does it work? Who would try it to find out? Alternatively rub raw garlic over the affected area. Apparently this can be quite effective but everybody knows where you are and steers well clear of you.

Perhaps warts are afflicting you. These are nasty little beasts that need severe treatment so why not try dandelions? Pull a dandelion from your yard, break the stem and squeeze some of its liquid onto your wart. Do this daily as needed. The juice is irritating, so it encourages your immune system to attack the wart. This remedy can be so aggravating that you can't stop scratching. If that doesn't work try birch bark! Dampen the bark with water and tie it over the wart with the inner side of the bark touching the skin. Alternatively dry some birch bark and powder it with a pestle and mortar then soak a teaspoon of powdered bark in a cup of boiling water for ten minutes, let it cool, soak a cloth in the liquid and press it on the wart. By the time all this has been done the warts have probably given up and disappeared. But if they haven't vanished try crushing fresh basil leaves and taping them over the warts. You must replace the leaves every day for up to a week.

Fruit and vegetables we are told are good for us but they are not all totally beneficial as they can cause flatulence. The main culprits are beans and cabbage and cauliflower and broccoli and onions and prunes and raisins and sprouts and pears and apples and…the list goes on. But do not despair. A remedy is within your reach! Simply grate some ginger and leave it in boiled water for about five minutes and then sip it. If you cannot face drinking a ginger infusion, then the simplest thing to do is just take a slice of ginger, bite it, chew it and swallow it. Ginger is a powerful so be ready for a hot surprise. And if ginger is not an appealing cure then try chewing fennel seeds. These can be effective and also cure bad breath.

Groundsel has a wonderful variety of alleged benefits and it has been much used for poultices and is regarded as good for sickness of the stomach. A weak infusion of the plant is sometimes thought to be a simple and easy purgative and a strong emetic. It causes no irritation or pain, removes bilious trouble and is regarded as a great cooler. In The Forest groundsel also had a reputation for curing boils. These uncomfortable red lumps filled with pus are very painful and can pop out in a variety of places on the body. Some would say a boil on the backside is especially painful and annoying as there is no easy way of sitting comfortably. For some reason boils once afflicted several families in Whytteford at the same time. Rural remedies were tested with varying degrees of failure. These included the use of bacon rind, eggs, onions, corn meal, parsley leaves, bread, garlic, nutmeg and even the infusion of groundsel. Eventually, despite the various 'cures' the spate of boils eased and the afflicted villagers re-discovered the joy of sitting comfortably.

Poor Mrs Moorson suffered from a sudden skin inflammation that stretched down the left of her face. From the right she looked perfectly well but the other side of her face had an angry red weal that even began to swell. When she saw Doctor Rundell he prescribed a soothing ointment that took away some of the burning sensation but it did not bring about a cure. Indeed the inflammation was gradually spreading over Mrs Moorson's face.

Once a year the gypsies would visit the villages of the area. They'd settle on common lands with their little horse-drawn wooden caravans, put their animals out to graze and carry on their trades of bodging, woodwork, fencing, ditching, selling bunches of heather that bring good luck and fortune telling. They were regular visitors and everybody knew them. When they moved on the only signs of their occupation were cropped turf and blackened patches where their fires had burnt.

Mrs Moorson's inflammation was not responding to any treatment and she didn't know what to do. When she heard a knocking at her door she was reluctant to answer but good manners prevailed and she was greeted by a brown-faced elderly gypsy woman with a basket of white heather in neat bunches. The gypsy stared at Mrs Moorson and immediately began talking.

'My dear,' she said, 'what ever has happened to you?'

'I don't know. I really don't know what it is and nothing seems to help it.'

'Well, my dear,' said the gypsy woman, 'would you let me have a look at it closely, really closely?'

The gypsy took Mrs Moorson into the garden and sat her on a bench where the sun shone. She peered closely and even sniffed at the diseased skin. This went on for several long moments then the gypsy stepped back.

'My dear,' she said, 'I do know a cure but I'll tell you now, you won't like it.'

'What is it? I'm desperate. My face often feels as if it's on fire.'

'Then you must do this. Go into your garden tonight and gather some snails.'

'Snails? What am I to do with the snails?'

'Nothing that will hurt you. Gather the snails and wipe them over your skin so that the slime covers up all the redness.'

'How will that help?'

'Don't ask that, just trust me. Start doing it tonight, before you go to bed and repeat it in the morning. I promise you that you'll soon be better.' The gypsy woman was so concerned about Mrs Moorson that she forgot to sell her a sprig of heather. 'I'll be back to see you in a couple of weeks.'

'Gather the snails and wipe them over your skin…'

The gypsy left and Mrs Moorson reluctantly did as she was told. It wasn't very nice wiping moist snails over her skin but she found doing this strangely soothing. After two days the burning sensations had eased. At the end of a week the inflammation had subsided and a few days later all that was left was a pale pink patch.

True to her word the gypsy woman called again.

'I told you snails would work for you,' she said the

moment Mrs Moorson opened the door of her cottage.

'I don't know how I can ever thank you,' said Mrs Moorson who was truly grateful.

'That's easy, my dear,' said the gypsy lady, 'just cross my palm with silver.'

'I will, I will,' said Mrs Moorson, and she gave the gypsy more silver than she was normally given in a day.

'Thank you, my dear,' said the gypsy, 'I'll see you again next year.'

'Come and see me whenever you are passing.'

'I will, my dear, indeed I will.' The gipsy lady's eyes twinkled. 'And then you can cross my palm with silver again.'

A Skimpy Victory

When Joe and Bessie were married everyone in Whytteford knew that they were very much in love. Bessie was very proud of Joe. He was kindly, loving, tall and handsome. She loved it when he took her in his sports car to quiet parts of The Forest where their open air loving would not be disturbed. And Joe was very proud of Bessie, who was good humoured and utterly devoted to him. She looked beautiful and wherever they went her shapely body and aura of sexuality drew many admiring glances and smiles. A few months after the wedding there was no sign of Bessie being pregnant. This was regarded as rather odd as many of the people of The Forest were grandparents before they were forty.

'Everythin' ollright?' Joe was asked in The Cobblers Arms one evening.

'Foine,' said Joe. 'Why do you arsk?'

'Your Bessie ollright?'

'Course she is, why shouldn't she be?'

'No soign of a littl'un on the way yet?'

'Plenty of toime for that,' said Joe, who did not like others prying into his affairs. 'Bessie's only twenny, lots of things for us to do before we 'ave a family.' Suddenly Joe's gentle voice became very sharp. 'Now that's that!' he snapped and the other regulars at The Cobblers realised that they mustn't ask anything more.

For the older generation Bessie and Joe's approach to marriage was odd but the young couple really did not care. Times were changing and many newlyweds did not rush to have children as they wanted some life together before adding the responsibility of children to their marriage. As a result Bessie's trim figure remained as delightful as ever.

Joe played cricket for the Whytteford team and Bessie supported him and helped with the match teas. She would produce delicious cakes but seldom tasted them herself.

'Have a piece of this chocolate cake, Bessie,' Jeb Carpenter, the team captain said one day. 'It's delicious.'

'I don't think I will, Jeb,' Bessie replied. 'I've got to watch my figure.'

'Ah!' said Jeb. 'Oi've been watching it all afternoon as well.'

The summer after Joe and Bessie were married was blisteringly hot. A glorious June was interrupted in the middle of the month by a prolonged storm then the sunshine shone every day until the end of September. Bessie loved the sunny weather. She wore pretty little sundresses that made her look delightful and the sunshine had made her hair an even lighter shade of blond. Joe was immensely proud of his pretty young wife and he loved it when she served opposing cricket teams with cake and sandwiches, gathering much admiration in the process.

The Whytteford team performed exceptionally well that summer losing few matches and reaching the final of The Forest Cricket League. The final match was against Hindbury, a formidable team by rural standards. Cricket in The Forest was unconventional at any time. Animals usually had to be driven from a pitch before a match could begin and rabbits had often made their burrows in unexpected places causing many an unwary fielder to fall down at a crucial moment. The strokes the batsmen used were unconventional too, being more akin to hedging and scything than the style of a professional cricketer. Bowlers also had their quirks, often barely bothering to take a run up yet somehow delivering the ball with immense speed.

The match against Hindbury did not go well. Captain Jeb Carpenter was in despair when the interval began and even Joe was despondent, as he had been caught out before he had even scored a dozen runs. The Whytteford team had been dismissed for just sixty-nine runs and defeat seemed inevitable. As the tea interval came to a close Joe could be seen having a word with Bessie.

'We don't stand a chance,' he muttered.

'Don't be silly,' said Bessie. 'The match isn't lost yet. Just concentrate on your bowling and you'll be surprised what happens.' There was a gleam in Bessie's eyes that gave Joe hope.

'What you'm got in mind?' he asked.

'Concentrate on your bowling and tell the others to concentrate too.'

Bessie continued serving and whenever a member of the Hindbury team was at the table she'd bend well forward as she passed a slice of cake and also gave each player enticing glimpses of her bronzed breasts. Her natural tan was clearly totally complete.

Joe had a brief chat with Jeb who then tried to encourage the Whytteford team finishing with, 'Now just concentrate; concentrate on the match!'

Hindbury began their innings with the first two batsmen developing a good partnership and scoring thirty-one runs before one of them was dismissed. As the next batsman walked to the wicket Bessie strolled from the pavilion in her little summer dress and carrying a cushion and a rug that she had collected from Joe's car. Although it was early evening the sun was shining with exceptional power and the air was warm. She spread the rug, placed the cushion at one end then stood watching the match. The eyes of the Hindbury batsmen were soon diverted in Bessie's direction. When Joe was about to bowl Bessie calmly undid some bows on the shoulders of her dress and it slid down to reveal that underneath was a tiny and enticing bikini. Bessie began sunbathing and nobody could stop her.

'Concentrate!' said Jeb and the Whytteford players obeyed their captain's orders.

Joe bowled directly at the stumps but for some reason the Hindbury batsman didn't keep his eye on the ball.

The middle stump was knocked out and Joe began to feel a little optimistic. Whenever Joe was bowling Bessie would work her magic. She would sit up to watch what was going on, she would stretch her arms and occasionally even stand up. During one over she slowly walked to where Joe's car was parked, collected a cool drink, and then calmly returned to her rug.

Bessie would sit up and watch what was going on…

The Hindbury batsmen, concentration gone, struggled to connect with the ball and gradually their wickets fell. Even the captain's innings ended on just three runs as when Joe began bowling to him Bessie suddenly jumped up and called out, 'Come on Joe!' Hindbury struggled to reach fifty but the last two batsmen battled valiantly and took the score to sixty. Just as the match seemed to be turning Hindbury's way Bessie stood up and put her dress back on, slowly covering the delights that had so distracted the visiting team. This subtle move proved too much. Joe bowled and as the batsman vainly tried to focus on the ball it whistled down the pitch and flew at the stumps with such force that the bails flew high into the air. One landed over the boundary and the other disappeared in to some bushes. The final score was Whytteford sixty-nine, Hindbury sixty-seven.

'Congratulations,' the Hindbury captain said to Jeb Carpenter. 'You had a skimpy victory but a victory nevertheless.'

The Whytteford celebrations went on through the hot summer evening but after a time Bessie and Joe were absent. 'Take me to our glade,' she had whispered to him. 'I'm so proud of you.'

The Jolly Butcher

Tucked away in Dragon Street, Humbury, was a special butcher's shop. Above the window could be seen a sign that read 'Elijah Jones, Family Butcher'. The term 'family butcher' has a certain sinister quality but Elly, as he was always called, would never have butchered any family. He was so kindly, happy and humorous that it was quite clear that there was never an evil or menacing thought in his mind. He spoke with a musicality that only the Welsh can give to English.

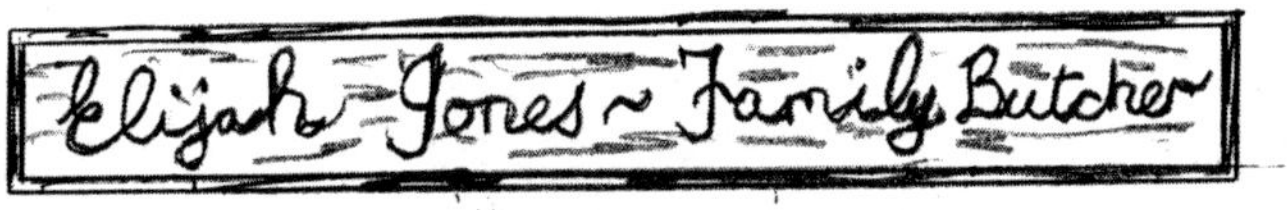

'Family butcher…'

The window of the shop was inviting as it was full of the finest meats that Elijah could sell. Cascades of home-made sausages hung from hooks together with rabbits and pheasants that were fresh from The Forest. As you approached the shop a truck might draw up. The driver would climb out, reach into the back and grab a pole on the end of which would be fresh game that had been killed and prepared in the last few hours. Inside the butcher's shop was a counter for cooked meats; up above hung cured hams and sides of bacon. Dishes of interesting pâtés were invitingly displayed including some made from the game of The Forest. Home-made pork pies with shining bronzed pastry were on display. If you bought one of these and ate it you soon discovered that on top of the pork was a layer of apple. The golden glossy pastry was firm but would cut lightly or your teeth would sink into it with ease. Beneath the apple was a delicious pork and herb mixture made from the best meat that Elly could choose.

Whatever you needed then Elijah would supply it. Venison was always available in The Forest if you knew who to ask but good venison could be in short supply. Elijah could always supply quality meat of any type, provided he was given sufficient notice. As popular car ownership increased, tourists, who came to Humbury to enjoy its timeless charm, often found Elly's distinctive butcher's shop with its special delights. Many would leave with pork pies and specially blended sausages but his best seller was the sausages he made from venison.

The people of Humbury and the many villages of the area came to Elijah's shop for more than his fine meat, pies, pâtés and sausages. They patronised the shop because of Elly himself. Always smiling, always happy, he would cheer up the most downhearted of customers. His cheery disposition and ready humour brought him regular customers who revelled in his joviality as much as they delighted in his meats, even though his witticisms could be double-edged. But, whatever he said with his cheeky wisecracks Elly was never malicious. He was just a jolly jester.

'Don't sit your backside on the bacon slicer,' he'd say. 'We don't want to get behind with the orders.' It was an old joke repeated many times but the customers still laughed as Elly was laughing with them.

'Now then, Elly,' said my good friend Elsie, 'I won't need any meat next week. I'm going off.'

'I'm sorry to hear that,' Elijah said with a twinkle in his eye. 'Going off are you? Well, I hadn't smelt anything.'

Requests from all were met with humoured courtesy...

Mrs Sponder, a lady of considerable bulk who made the bench of the Whytteford Church harmonium creak and groan every time she mounted it, had an unfortunate turn of phrase. She would often comment on the fortunes of life, 'Well, I'm sure destiny shapes our ends.' Many a time she would use this expression and if there was a queue in Elijah's shop he might hear it several times in a few minutes. Smiles would break out over his face and his mouth would begin gently working and he would struggle to control his words.

Eventually Mrs Sponder used, 'Well, I'm sure destiny shapes our ends,' so many times that as her substantial rear end left his shop Elly called out, 'Well it didn't make a very good job of yours, did it?' Mrs Sponder turned round slowly. Elly wondered if he had gone too far with his ready humour. And then Mrs Sponder suddenly exploded in a guffaw of laughter that could be heard all along Dragon Street!

One of Elijah's customers was called Mrs Parslee. She was a regular customer and always in good humour. He always greeted her courteously and would ask, as she was about to leave, 'By the way, Mrs Parslee, have you got the time?'

And then Mrs Parslee would leave the shop.

'Why do you always ask her for the time?' another regular customer asked one day.

'Well,' said Elly in his lilting Welsh tones, 'parsley and thyme usually go together.'

Requests from all were met with humoured courtesy.

'I would like some nice steak for this evening, please, Elly,' a pretty young lady might say.

'Giving your boyfriend something special, are you?'

'I thought I'd give him a treat.'

'I expect he'll enjoy the steak as well. Come back later if you need stuffing.'

'Some stewing steak for my grandpa please.'

'Cook it on a low heat for three hours and then he won't need to put his teeth in.'

Waiting in the queue one day I enjoyed the gentle teasing and badinage that was exchanged between the butcher and his customers. Everyone left with a smiling face and a packet of quality meat, or another item of Elly's special produce.

Two places in front of me was Mrs Landy, who had been to Humbury for her weekly shop.

'Now then, Elly,' said Mrs Landy, 'do you keep dripping?'

Elly looked about the shop, then down at his feet .

'I don't think so,' he said, and then he looked up. 'The floor is perfectly dry.'

Off To Court...

The official looking letter began with the words, 'You are summonsed to...' what was all this about? What had I done? Where had I done it? How had my crime been perpetrated? How had it been discovered? I read the rest of the letter. I had been called for jury service at Salchester Crown Court and there was no escape.

The day came and I arrived at the court together with nineteen other potential jurors. The clerk of the court met us in a quiet room and explained our duties concluding with the statement that twelve of us would soon be in court. Eventually we were ushered into the jury box and several jurors were rejected on behalf of the defendants. This is something that does not happen today. We had been told that we must look at the defendants in case they were known to us but I had never seen any of them before. Eventually enough jurors had been accepted and we were sworn in. Some of the jurors were understandably nervous as they read the oath.

'I,..., do swear by Almighty God that I will well and truly serve our Sovereign Lady Queen Elizabeth the Second...'

The problem word was 'sovereign'. One juror held up the petite Bible each of us had been given and swore the oath in a good clear tone. Unfortunately 'Sovereign Lady' became 'Foreign Lady' but this was ignored. As I took the oath I realised that my voice had suddenly become several tones higher than normal but the Queen was safe on her throne. The next juror had given no indication of communist leanings but his oath was to 'our Soviet Lady'. To my amusement this too was ignored and the case proceeded.

I found the whole process fascinating. The main defendant had been ordered to keep away from his former wife, her family and their children. But one night, just before Christmas, he had decided to travel well over a hundred miles from London, break into their home at two o'clock in the morning and take his children away. He had two accomplices; his brother who always looked as if he was about to fall asleep, and a cheeky looking friend who was always bouncing up and down in the dock.

As the case proceeded over the next few days we learnt a lot about these people. The principle defendant had married a girl and had had two children with her. But she had a twin sister and he had had a child with her as well. They may have been twins but one was slender and the other was fulsome. It was not as though he had woken in the night, gone to the lavatory and returned to the wrong bed without realising what he was doing! The more buxom twin could not be mistaken for her sister even on a pitch black night. What was his secret that two girls from the same family had found him so irresistible?

The judge was a delight. I was quite envious of his red and blue robes. Each time he appeared he bowed to us all and gave a regal wave prior to taking his seat. He carried some gloves that were placed on the bench and then he looked over his glasses and addressed whichever barrister was due to speak. His Honour spoke clearly and we had no trouble understanding a word he said. There were humorous moments, but really that is an understatement as there were also moments of hilarity.

There was the detail that the father of the non-identical twins insisted on including in his evidence. He was determinedly correct in all that he said.

'Would you tell the jury what happened in the early hours of the morning of the 19th of December?' asked the prosecuting barrister.

'We couldn't sleep so I said I was going to make a cup of tea. But I didn't.'

'What did you do?' asked the barrister.

We all hung on the father's words expecting him to

describe a dramatic interruption.

'I decided to make hot chocolate.'

'And when you made the hot chocolate what did you do?'

'I returned to bed and me and the wife drunk it and we were soon asleep.'

'And was your sleep interrupted at all?'

'No it wasn't.'

'Not at all?'

'Not until we heard the front door slam.'

'And why did it slam?'

'Because someone had shut it with a bang.'

'Why do you think it banged?'

'Because the person who shut it was in a hurry.'

'Did you hear anything else?'

'Yes I did.'

'What did you hear?'

'I heard a car being revved up, then the car door slammed and it roared away.'

'Why do you think the people in the car were in such a hurry?'

'Because the people in it had just taken away my grandchildren.'

One of the accused spoke rapidly with a strong north London accent. 'The police said they'ad trouble unnerstandin me. Idunno why they'ad trouble as nobdy'eretoday seems to'ave'ad anytrouble unnerstandin me.'

The judge visibly rose in his throne-like chair and glowered at the defendant. The jury quailed before him but the defendant seemed totally oblivious of the judge's mood.

The judge visibly rose in his throne-like chair and he glowered at the defendant.

'Mr Rotham. I for one have had considerable difficulty in understanding you.' His words resounded in the courtroom then he looked at the jury box, clearly seeking approbation. We dutifully laughed and nodded our heads. 'And it seems that the members of the jury agree with me.'

Eventually we had heard all the evidence and the arguments. His Honour gave an eloquent summary and we retired to the Jury Room. This had a lavatory and a clanking extractor. We were not allowed to open any windows as that side of the court building was next to the street. Of the twelve jurors only two did not smoke. We couldn't use the fan because it was so noisy that we could not discuss the case. The atmosphere became thick with the smell of burning tobacco and I suspect that I inhaled more cigarette smoke that day than I have in the rest of my life. My clothes smelt and although we could claim certain expenses dry cleaning was not included.

Were the defendants guilty or not guilty? I must not report any of the deliberations that we had in the Jury Room but they were all found guilty. The case took five days and cost thousands of pounds. The sentences seemed minimal for the crimes committed as the family had been terrorised for some time, but the judge could do no more. Nevertheless he made his opinion clear by his words and his tone. 'Official guidelines tell me what is considered an appropriate sentence, and I am obliged to follow those guidelines.' He glowered at the defendants and gave sentences ranging from a few weeks to eighteen months. I sensed that he would have liked the sentences to have been measured in years!

Lionel And Elsie's Cleaner

Whenever I visited Elsie and Lionel I knew that I would be well entertained. Usually I was invited for coffee but this always became a large glass of gin and tonic with clinking ice cubes and a slice of lemon. I didn't know what Lionel's secret was but the drinks he served always tasted better than anyone else's.

'What's your secret?' I asked one day.

'Nothing special,' he replied.

'What type of gin is it?'

'Nothing special.'

'Do you use a different type of tonic?'

'No, nothing special?'

That was all he would say and I was kept puzzled.

Elsie and Lionel had two cats that were a law unto themselves. They'd wander in and out and the only time they were regularly seen was when food was on offer. Ben was a tortoiseshell and the other cat, Archie, was a curious rich bronze colour that made him look quite distinguished in a feline manner.

As well as the delights of Lionel's special drinks and the good humour that they both had there was their zest for life that many younger people seemed to lack. Elsie had a wide range of interests and she was always busy. As she grew older she was determined to make the most of life and let others do the things that she found tiresome or wearing.

'We are going to have a cleaner,' she announced one day. 'I'm far too busy to waste my time cleaning the house. I'm not giving up my art or my gardening or bridge parties or my cooking.' I understood her reasoning. Elsie was an accomplished artist, a superb, inventive cook and no doubt an expert bridge player. Elsie and Lionel worked together in their garden that was always colourful whatever the season.

Finding a cleaner was not easy even though they were

willing to pay generously. A notice in the village shop produced no replies and so Elsie arranged for a small advertisement to be placed in the Humbury Advertiser.

This local newspaper had articles about ploughing matches, village shows, church fetes, weddings, funerals and local court reports. Country newspapers covered topics that would never be included in a city paper. In one issue it was reported that someone had been fined for having a faulty rear light, an escaped pig had caused a hold-up on the road from Humbury to Salchester and that the council had decided to redecorate the town hall. Wedding reports were accompanied by photographs of the bride and groom together and sometimes with guests surrounding them. One such account described the bride's dress and the costumes of the bridesmaids but when the bride's mother's outfit was described there was room for just one sentence that read; 'The bride's mother wore a blue hat.'

This tickled Lionel's sense of humour and he showed me the report with a huge smile on his face and his eyes twinkling. 'Is that all she wore? It must have been a very unusual wedding.'

The advertisement for a cleaner produced one response. A lady who lived in Humbury telephoned Elsie and enquired about the job. A few days later a figure wearing a broad-brimmed hat with an outsized, long coat cycled from Humbury to Whytteford on an elderly and rusty bicycle that was in great need of oiling, maintenance and new tyres. She dismounted and wheeled the machine up the drive to Elsie and Lionel's house. To Lionel's great disgust she propped the bicycle against his car and then removed her gloves and stuffed them into the pockets of her capacious coat. She then dithered outside the door as if she didn't know what to do.

Elsie had been watching through a side window and she was annoyed by this prevarication. As the lady was about to knock on the front door Elsie opened it so energetically that the woman stood open-mouthed with an expression somewhere between puzzlement and amazement on her face. Her jaw opened and shut several times but she did not speak.

'Hello,' said Elsie, 'are you here about the advertisement?'

'Y…e…e…s,' the woman drawled. She didn't stutter or stumble.

'You'd better come in,' Elsie continued, 'come in and tell me about yourself.'

'Y…e…e…s.'

The lady went in and stood in the hall as Elsie tried to lead her into the kitchen but she didn't move.

'Come in here.'

'Y…e…e…s.'

'All I want you to do is general cleaning. Is that all right?

'Y…e…e…s.'

'You may find I've left you a pile of washing up after I have been cooking. I expect you to clean everything for me. You will do that, won't you?'

'Y…e…e…s.'

'Can you start next week?'

'Y…e…e…s.'

'That's good. Tuesdays would suit us. Would that suit you?'

'Y…e…e…s.'

'Very well, we'll see you next week.'

'Y…e…e…s.'

'Could you tell me your name?'

'Y…e…e…s.'

'Well…?'

'Erm…er…' Elsie began to wonder if the woman knew her own name. 'Kitty I am…er…Kitty.'

And the next Tuesday she began to work. She wasn't quick but she was thorough and whatever Elsie asked

Kitty to do was eventually done.

'She's driving me round the twist,' Lionel told me one day.

'Not that anyone has noticed,' interjected Elsie.

'I can't find a blooming thing after she's been. She doesn't tidy up; she moves things all over the place.' Lionel was clearly unhappy.

'But there was nobody else,' said Elsie.

After a while Kitty began to do extra things. On the hottest day she decided to clean all the windows on the sunny side of the house and then complained about the heat. In the winter, on a bitter frosty morning, she put some washing on the line and wondered why it froze in the cold air.

'I don't know why we have her,' grumbled Lionel. 'She's bonkers.'

'She's all we could find,' Elsie muttered. 'I'm sick of housework when I can do far more important things.'

A few weeks later I was visiting Elsie and Lionel for 'coffee' and enjoying an appetising gin and tonic when Lionel began to talk about Kitty.

'Our amazing cleaner has surpassed herself.'

'Has she been working well?' I asked.

'She certainly has!' Elsie declared with a more than a hint of asperity. 'She's been working so well that we have finished with her.'

'What on earth had she done?'

'It was last Tuesday morning and Kitty was due but we were just going out. Archie suddenly returned from a hunting expedition.'

'He was carrying a dead rat,' explained Elsie.

'Horrific thing,' said Lionel, 'quite revolting; really hairy with a long tail.'

'We were aghast.' Elsie shuddered as she spoke.

'I managed to get it off him, put it on an old newspaper and left it on a bench in the garage.'

'Kitty arrived and off we went,' said Elsie, 'and never

gave that rat another thought.'

'When we got back dear Kitty had gone and we decided it was time for gin and tonic,' said Lionel, 'and I went to the garage to bring in some more bottles of tonic.'

'We just keep tonic in the garage,' added Elsie, 'the gin is kept in a much safer place.'

'I went to the garage and passed the bench and realised the rat wasn't there. It should have been flat on the newspaper, but they'd both gone.'

'I managed to get it off him, put it on an old newspaper and left it on a bench in the garage.'

'Lionel came in and told me the rat had vanished. I

suggested that one of the cats had taken it, but it was nothing to do with them.'

'Anyway,' said Lionel, 'I started mixing the gin and tonic and I suddenly saw a note on top of the trolley.'

'That's when we knew that Kitty was never going to work for us again,'

I sat waiting to hear what the note had said but both Elsie and Lionel were taking large gulps of gin and tonic.

'I still can't believe it,' said Elsie. 'I shudder every time I think about it.'

'What was written on the note?'

'You won't believe it,' said Elsie.

'It said…' and Lionel paused to drink some more gin and tonic, 'rat in fridge!'

The Harmonium

The music at Whytteford church wheezed, puffed and oozed from an ancient harmonium that was so old that my grandfather, who was born in 1887, told me that it had been a feature of the church when he was young and his father had told him that it was very, very old. Every Sunday Mrs Sponder heaved her considerable bulk on to the bench, pumped heavily with her feet and began to play the music chosen for the service. The seat creaked and grumbled as Mrs Sponder exerted herself and semi-musical sounds emerged from the harmonium. At least I presumed they came from the instrument but I also wondered if some of the windy noises may have been the result of Mrs Sponder's efforts. Nobody would have realised as the harmonium was no longer capable of producing any truly tuneful sounds. Mrs Sponder had limited musical abilities and however hard she tried to vary tunes and tempos every hymn that she played sounded virtually the same. There was a combination of puffing, woozing and off-key whistling that combined with the squeaks and groans that came from the straining wood of the seat meant that no tune was easily identifiable. Fortunately most of the hymns chosen were well known to the congregation and so despite Mrs Sponder's dubious efforts services usually progressed with the singers leading the music rather than following the lead given by Mrs Sponder.

The harmonium was well past its prime…

Undoubtedly the harmonium was well past its prime. The range of temperatures that it endured would not have helped. The church, tucked away in a valley, was cool on the hottest summer days. In the winter it was always cold and often for several days the temperature inside the building did not rise above freezing point. There was an ancient tortoise stove that old Harry, who acted as verger, would light up if there was a service but this only warmed the air nearby. The windows remained rhymed by frost and the air bitterly cold. On one Christmas morning the entire congregation's breath was visible as everyone attempted to sing joyful carols.

Eventually the harmonium, having suffered an unfavourable climate for well over a century and struggled under the burden of Mrs Sponder, gave up. It was on a Saturday morning that she went to the little Saxon church to practise the hymns for the next day. Having clambered on to the groaning bench Mrs Sponder pumped through 'Our God our help in ages past' and then moved on to the next hymn. The first verse seemed to go quite well but in the second verse a peculiar puff and whoosh of stale air and unmusical sounds made it plain that the harmonium had played its final offering and it would not be accompanying the service the next day.

Mrs Sponder pedalled to the rectory on her antiquated bicycle. This took some time as the journey was two miles, the road had a slight hill and she was not accustomed to bicycling such great distances. It was a tired, breathless and red-faced Mrs Sponder who tugged on the bell next to the rectory door. She heard the barking of two dogs and the sound of the rector's voice and then the Reverend Phillip Paston opened the door. The sight that greeted him made him gasp in amazement but he soon took control of himself.

'Why, Mrs Sponder, whatever is the matter?'

'The…the…har…har…' She was trying to say harmonium but all she could manage was 'Har…har…har.'

This meant little to the rector. 'Come in and have a cup of tea and tell me about it,' he said.

Fortunately there was a rail next to the steps to the rectory door. Mrs Sponder somehow pulled herself up the steps and the rector guided her to the lounge and she subsided into a capacious armchair. Here she sat puffing after all the exertions she had put herself through and gradually her face changed from a glowing red to a radiant pink. Meanwhile the rector had made a pot of tea and he strode into the room with the tea tray and a plate of home-made cakes.

'Now what's the problem?' he asked solicitously. 'Do have some tea and help yourself to the cakes.'

Mrs Sponder told her tale puffing as loudly as the ancient harmonium and the rector listened attentively. He had a gentle smile on his face that Mrs Sponder found very reassuring. In fact the rector was amused to see that the cakes were quickly slipping down Mrs Sponder's throat as she relaxed and drank several cups of tea.

'Now there's no need to worry,' he said when she had finished her tale. 'I am sure we can manage.'

The rector phoned several of the villagers who played instruments and put together a church band which performed at the services for the next few weeks. Having suffered considerable strain for many years the harmonium was beyond repair. Fortunately the church funds were sufficient to purchase a small Victorian organ and in time it was installed in place of the harmonium and Mrs Sponder settled down to some serious practice. Eventually she announced that she was ready to play at a service. As the congregation arrived she meandered through a gentle tune but after the rector had given words of welcome it was time for the first hymn. It was perhaps unfortunate that the first hymn for the service, and indeed the first hymn Mrs Sponder played on the organ, was 'Fight the good fight' as battle certainly ensued. The congregation sang as lustily as ever but they were not following the organ and the organist was not following the congregation. Really they did not notice any difference between the sounds that had come from the discarded harmonium and the reverberations emerging from the organ created by Mrs Sponder's inexpert fingers.

Truth has to be told. Despite her practising Mrs Sponder was struggling to master the organ and although her fingers attempted to play something resembling the tune they were not moving as quickly as they should. By the end of the third verse the congregation was well ahead of the organ. Not used to having any strong lead from an instrument they sung on gathering speed a little as they warbled. Eventually the last verse was reached and the final lines were sung but as the congregation finished the organ continued to play. Mrs Sponder gradually came to the end of a verse and then ploughed into what she regarded as the concluding stanza. Almost deafened by the power of the organ she had not realised that the congregation had finished the hymn and was beginning to sit down. Hearing another verse commence many of the people in the church hovered over their seats then stood and began the last verse once more. The singing from the congregation was inevitably weaker as there was an edge of uncertainty and the organ reverberated through the church drowning out the weakened voices until at last the final line of the hymn was reached for the second time.

What A Way To Go!

On the southern edge of The Forest is Brockswarth House which is owned by the Earl of Melcaster. It's lovely to visit this elegant Georgian mansion approaching through spacious parkland that is surrounded by an estate of about two thousand acres. Often guests who stayed at our home were keen to discover Brockswarth and occasionally I went with them to enjoy the gardens and to marvel at the splendid rooms.

On one occasion as we walked to the entrance a family with a young girl were just ahead of us.

'Enjoy your visit,' the lady in the ticket office said.

'Did Queen Elizabeth ever stay here?' asked the girl.

'No dear, the present house wasn't built when Queen Elizabeth was alive.'

'Was there another house then?'

'There was a Tudor mansion and the queen did pass this way.'

'Did she stay in that house?'

'Queen Elizabeth I did pass by in 1572 but she didn't stay here.'

'Why didn't she stay? Didn't she like the earl?'

'The roads were very bad and her great progress was several weeks behind schedule.'

'Did the earl ask her to stay here?'

'The earl was delighted that she didn't stay. A visit by the queen and all her followers could cost a lot of money.'

'How much..?

'Come along Eleanor,' said the girl's father. 'That's enough questions for now.'

The family moved on and we bought our tickets and followed Eleanor and her entourage.

The first great house was built by the second Earl of Melcaster in the middle of the sixteenth century and his descendants live there to this day. Brockswarth House has remained on the edge of history without anything important ever happening there. Stately homes have frequently welcomed visitors but nowadays tourism is big business and few survive without the benefit of thousands of visitors who tour great houses and gardens, search for photographs of 'the family', eat many cakes and scones and spend money on curiosities and oddities in the inevitable shop.

As we went into the house Eleanor was just in front of us and she took a lively interest in everything that she was told.

The architecture of Brockswarth House is excellent and the plasterwork ceilings are truly memorable. You see dignified portraits of ancient earls and countesses staring down at the hoi polloi that pass through the rooms, never straying beyond little gilt posts supporting plaited ropes. In each room is a steward who will keenly answer any questions. Some are so keen that they do not wait for questions to be asked.

As soon as we entered the marble hall the steward pounced and immediately introduced us to the history of Brockswarth. She pointed to an oil painting that depicted the seventh earl on horseback.

A portrait of the seventh earl on horseback…

'This is Gerald, the seventh earl, who built the present house. He was an enthusiastic horseman although sadly it was riding that caused his death. The earl was on his favourite mount, Raven, a startlingly black horse hence the name. The earl loved to jump fences but unfortunately on that November day the ground was slippery, after heavy overnight rain. The horse slipped, bucked and threw the earl over a fence, he fell badly and broke several bones. He was conscious but a sudden downpour of rain showered him and his temperature fell rapidly, a fever developed and he died. Does anybody have a question?'

'Did the horse live?' asked Eleanor.

'I don't know the answer to that. Now would you please move on to the dining room?'

We shuffled through and another steward greeted us. 'You are now in the dining room.' This was a rather obvious statement as the table was laid for a banquet with fine porcelain, cut glass and silver cutlery in abundance. What other room could it be? Items were described and details pointed out but as we moved on to the drawing room we would pass the great stairway.

'As you pass the great stairs look up to the landing and you will see a picture of Raven, the seventh earl's favourite horse. In fact it was Raven that caused the seventh earl's death. The earl was standing on the landing admiring the picture when he stepped backwards, caught his foot on the edge of the stair carpet, and fell head over heels down the stairs, broke his neck and died immediately. He was succeeded by his son, Montagu, who became the eighth earl. Since that day the earls have never used that stairway, nor have their visitors.'

'Was the carpet damaged?' Eleanor seemed to be asking questions that no other visitor had ever considered.

'If you look carefully you will see that the carpet is in

perfect condition as it hasn't been used for over two hundred years.'

'How can we look if the stairway is never used?'

The steward was a little flustered by this question.

'Now move along and do look at the picture of Raven.'

We moved on passing the stairway and admiring Raven's portrait. As soon as we entered the drawing room the room steward smiled and welcomed us.

'You have just passed the splendid equestrian picture of Raven, the seventh earl's favourite horse. In fact Raven was the cause of the earl's demise. He was extremely pleased with the artist's painting and insisted on being involved with the hanging of the great picture. Two ladders were erected at the top of the stairway and the earl climbed one ladder whilst his son, Montagu, soon to become the eighth earl, climbed the other. They mounted the ladders together, hauling the picture on ropes as staff supported it from below. Unfortunately the earl's ladder slid on the carpet and fell down causing him to fall headlong down the stairs. He died almost instantly, just managing to say, "Fishing for salmon, Raven. Rav…en's gone fish…ing." Nobody knows quite what he meant by this strange remark.'

'Was the ladder broken?'

'I don't know the answer to that question. Now you are going to enter the library.' The confused steward waved us along rather urgently.

Eventually the tour was over and it was time for excellent scones, jam and cream. How did the seventh earl die? Did he fall off Raven? Did he fall down the stairs? Or did a slipping ladder cause his demise?

In the tearoom Eleanor was reading the freely available guide to Brockswarth House and saw that the picture of the seventh earl on Raven was featured.

'This is interesting,' said Eleanor, and in a very clear voice she read, 'Gerald, the seventh earl, died at the then considered great age of eighty-two in the dining room of Brockswarth House, having eaten a hearty meal.'

Happy Returns

The Whytteford and Chamford Girl Guides were organising a celebration. Miss Appleton had been leader of the troupe for forty years but she had decided it was time to retire. Such an event could not be allowed to pass unmarked and so guides from the past were contacted and although many knew what was planned everything had to be very hush-hush as Miss Appleton was not to know anything about the event.

Letters were sent throughout the country spreading the news. With each letter was a list of former guides who could not be contacted. Did anyone know where these ladies were living? Did anyone know if they were still alive? Long phone calls full of reminiscences were made and gradually a long list of old guides and some very old guides was created. Donations for a gift for Miss Appleton began to trickle in and the fund grew and grew. A date was fixed and many former guides announced that they would be attending. This posed another problem. How were all these guides to be accommodated? Although some had not moved very far others were travelling some distance. Who would be prepared to offer bed and breakfast to them? Some stayed at The Cobblers Arms, The Brown Bear and even at Mrs Stevenson's curious bed and breakfast accommodation.

When the great day arrived seemingly familiar faces from past times mingled with the local people and conversations about events in the past were discussed and argued over. Old friendships were reignited and past enmities remembered. The visitors rediscovered the bakery at Chamford and bought delicious bread and cakes.

There was a sweet shop in Humbury that had been run by Florrie Tasker for many years. She was always immaculately dressed but her face was smothered in far too much make-up. Foundation and powder were liberally applied together with some blusher that almost glowed as she moved about the little shop. Indeed, Florrie's cheeks were often as bright and shiny as the red layer discovered in a freshly sucked gob-stopper. Her eyebrows were black, eyelashes thickened with mascara and her lips were always an unsubtle gleaming red. The delights of Florrie's shop gave pleasure to generations of children as she always had delicious coconut ice, sherbet dabs and multi-coloured liquorice assortments. There were exciting chocolate bars and peppermint creams, gaudy lollipops, treats and pleasures for all ages. For over forty years Florrie had run her little shop and it had barely changed; nor had Florrie as she presented herself in just the same way for all those years. Inevitably, as the visitors chatted happily Florrie's little shop was mentioned.

'Do you remember the sweet shop in Humbury?'

'That must have closed years ago.'

'No, it's still there.'

'Who ran it? I can't remember her name.'

'That was Florrie. Florrie Tasker.'

'She must have been dead a few years now.'

'No she isn't. She's still running her little shop.'

'Good gracious. I used to love that shop. My grandfather used to give me a shilling and take me in there. I'll have to go and see it.'

'I'll come with you.'

And so two intrepid ex-girl guides drove into Humbury, parked in Dragon Street and tried to remember where they would find the sweet shop.

'I'm sure it's just down here.' They walked along Coster Street and there, on a corner, they saw the skewed timber-framed shop that looked as if it was about to fall down. It had always seemed slightly precarious and time had changed nothing.

They saw the skewed timber-framed shop that looked as if it was about to fall down…

'There it is. It's even smaller than I remembered.'

'Let's go in.'

The old doorbell jangled as it had for decades and Florrie bustled from her sitting room into the shop.

'Hello, my dears,' she said cheerily. 'What can I tempt you to today?' Florrie's greeting was the same as it had always been and she stood in her unchanging shop immaculately dressed and as imperfectly over made-up as she had ever been. She looked at her customers quizzically. 'Don't I know you?' she asked. 'Haven't I seen you before?'

The reminiscing customers explained why they were visiting.

'I remember such happy times in here.'

'That's very kind of you, dear,' said Florrie. 'Good of

you to come back and see me.'

'You haven't changed one bit.'

'No, you're exactly the same.'

Florrie was delighted.

'You've made my day!' she exclaimed. 'You haven't seen me for over twenty-five years and you say that to me. You've made my day!'

Halloween

When I was young Halloween was never mentioned or celebrated in any way. There were no parties, no carved pumpkins and no special Halloween party things for sale in the shops. Nobody minded walking past a graveyard on 31st October even if it was a damp and misty evening. If anyone had ventured past Whytteford church on that day the most alarming vision would have been old Harry who might have been tending some graves or digging a fresh one. Visiting the north of the country near the end of October one year I saw carved pumpkins for the first time and even asked what they were for.

'They're for Halloween.'

'What do you do with them?'

'We put a candle in each one and light it at dusk.'

'That must look nice,' I said.

'They're not meant to look nice. They're to frighten nasty things away.'

I wondered if one would have frightened Auntie Madge away.

Gradually the festivities of Halloween spread throughout the country and even reached The Forest. Children created pumpkin lanterns, put on peculiar costumes and enjoyed or were terrified at Halloween parties. 'Trick or treat' excursions began but in Whytteford only the homes near the centre of the village were visited. Ghosts, ghouls, zombies and witches seemed not to have enough strength to walk as far as the more remote cottages.

'I'm going trickle treating, tonight,' said one small boy to Lionel on one Halloween.

'Are you really?' asked Lionel. 'Don't you mean trick or treating?'

'No,' said the boy. 'Trickle treating!'

Lionel stood chuckling to himself as the boy went on his way.

I always enjoyed Lionel's infectious laughter and he was still laughing when I crossed the road to join him.

'What's so funny, Lionel?'

'Trick or treating is silly enough,' he said, 'but that boy absolutely insists that he's going trickle treating. I dread to think what will happen!'

'How's Elsie?' I asked.

'She's fine. Where have you been? We haven't seen you for ages.'

'I'm only a visitor to Whytteford now.'

'Well, come and join us for a bite this evening. Elsie would love to see you. I can provide better spirits than any that will be out and about at Halloween!'

By six o'clock we were enjoying Lionel's generous glasses of gin and tonic but Elsie seemed a little restless.

'What's all the fidgeting for?' asked Lionel.

'I just need to keep an eye on the cooking,' said Elsie. 'I'm preparing something special, in case we have any visitors.'

'Nobody else is coming, are they?'

'You never know,' Elsie said in a mysterious way, and she disappeared into the kitchen.

'I wonder what she's plotting,' Lionel muttered. 'She's up to something I can tell.'

Elsie returned a moment later looking totally calm and holding a besom broom.

'What are you doing?' Lionel asked. 'Why have you been out to the shed?'

'I'm getting a surprise ready in case we have any unwanted visitors,' said Elsie. Then she vanished into the hall and we heard her climbing the stairs.

'She's really plotting something,' muttered Lionel.

Elsie reappeared wearing a black cloak and holding the broom.

'What do I look like?' she asked.

'You look like you plan to sweep up leaves wearing a

velvet cloak,' Lionel replied. 'Pretty nutty if you ask me.'

'How about this then?' From behind her back Elsie produced a witch's hat with straggly black hair dangling from it. She popped it on her head and her portrait was complete. She looked like a witch. Lionel, who had been sipping his drink, suddenly spluttered.

'Good grief!' he said. 'You might have warned me!'

'You look wonderful,' I said. 'Are you going to a party?'

'I'm staying right here,' said Elsie, 'but if anyone comes knocking at our door tonight they'll encounter me dressed like this.'

'Let's hope the rector doesn't drop in,' murmured Lionel.

Elsie took off her disguise and seemed more relaxed.

'Where did you find that hat?' I asked.

'There's a fancy dress shop opened in Humbury. I saw it in the window and I couldn't resist it. I just hope we have some dear little callers.'

'If we do they won't call again,' said Lionel. 'They'll go running down the path before you can say hocus-pocus!'

Later that evening there was a sharp knocking on the front door and the bell was rung insistently.

'Trick or treat!' chorused the visitors. 'Trick or treat!'

In a moment Elsie had put on the cloak and hat.

There was more knocking and bell ringing. 'Trick or treat! Trick or treat!'

'I'm coming, my dears,' Elsie shouted in a very peculiar voice. 'I'm coming!'

She picked up the besom and opened the front door. An assortment of ghosts, a zombie, a wizard and two witches stood in front of her illuminated by the light in the porch.

'Trick or treat! Trick or tr…tr…tr…' The chorus faded away as the curious figures stared at Elsie.

'There you are, my dears!' she said in a cackling voice.

'I've been waiting for you.'

The collection of peculiar visitors stood still and remained silent.

'Now what can I do for you?'

'Trick or treat,' murmured a brave ghost.

'Trick or treat,' said Elsie, still speaking in her special voice. 'Then I'll give you a treat.' From inside the cloak she produced some little mandarin oranges and she gave them out. 'Be careful how you eat them. I've prepared them especially for you.'

'Th…thank you,' said the brave ghost.

'Th…thank you,' murmured his companions, and then they turned and fled down the path. Elsie rejoined us with a broad smile on her face.

'That was fun.'

'Why did you tell them to eat the mandarins carefully?' asked Lionel. 'They were just mandarins.'

'They were special mandarins.'

'What had you done to them?'

'I injected a little hot Tabasco sauce into them. That's my trick.'

'You old witch,' said Lionel. 'You really are an old witch!'

'You old witch,' said Lionel. 'You really are an old witch!'

A Walk In The Forest

The tranquillity of The Forest with the woodlands and countryside is relaxing and refreshing. Sunny glades, deep woods and stretches of open land relax any walker. Inevitably I moved away as work took me to other parts of the country. A visit to The Forest was like a holiday rest cure.

My constant delight was walking across the common land, revisiting favourite places and sometimes even discovering new delights. As well as happy memories of romance in quiet places there were spectacular views. Looking down to Standmoor Pool on a warm day was always a special sight as usually ponies would be grazing nearby, close cropping the turf and then drinking from the waters. On the hottest days cattle might be in the water drinking and cooling themselves before lumbering up the bank and then resting as they chewed the cud.

Walking further on I'd see Woodbine Wood in the distance and recall how great Auntie Mabel had become a little bemused by long distant memories when I had asked her about this place. The wood was remote from Whytteford and in the summer was popular with young lovers who enjoyed the serenity, the scent of wild honeysuckle and other delights. It was also a wonderful place for wildlife. In winter and summer the deer would shelter under the trees for protection from the heat or cold winds.

I was visiting The Forest late one summer and decided to have a ramble. I hadn't been to Stagstone Hill for ages and it was a favourite viewpoint. Really it was a small hill created in the Iron Age and so it suddenly rose from the earth in a quite flat area of The Forest. On one side it was fairly steep but there was a gentler slope that took visitors up to the summit and then Stagstone offered views over several miles. When I was young I could climb the hill and look back to Whytteford but after a few years birch trees had grown and blocked the view. I can remember being lost on one occasion but I climbed the hill and was able to work out where I had been and where I must go if I was to return home safely.

The late morning was bright and the sun was warm so instead of going directly to Stagstone Hill I decided to walk to Chamford, visit The Brown Bear, have a sandwich and a shandy for lunch, and then walk on to Stagstone. The company in The Brown Bear was good and one shandy became two. The conversation flowed and it seemed rude to refuse another drink.

Feeling very happy I eventually moved on and walked to Stagstone. I chose the gentle route to the summit and was soon enjoying the view that I hadn't seen for a while. Nature had done its work, some bushes and trees were bigger, one or two trees had fallen and quite a lot of silver birches had grown. But there were also gaunt skeletons in the woods. Birches are short-lived trees and a very dry summer two years beforehand had deprived them of water. These trees had given up and all that was left was silver trunks and the remains of boughs. As I surveyed the scene I could not help but notice clouds building up and a chilly breeze developing. It was time to complete my ramble and so I made my way down the hill, this time choosing the steeper and more direct path.

As I neared the base of the hill a natural urge began to build up. The third shandy at The Brown Bear was having an effect that could not be ignored. It was very quiet and nobody was in sight. I looked about and spotted a very secluded space among the gorse bushes. I carefully crept in and began to do what I had to do.

I had scarcely begun when I heard a buzzing sound in the distance. I thought it was probably somebody from one of the distant cottages doing some mowing so initially I took no notice. The sound seemed to be becoming louder and more insistent. What was it? By now I could not possibly stop what I was doing and the sound became more dominant yet the source remained invisible. Suddenly it was very close, in fact it was directly above me and so I looked up and saw a micro-light aircraft that was not very high. The pilot looking straight down at me as I looked straight up at him. I am not sure which of us was the more surprised! After all, neither of us could stop what we were doing!

I heard a buzzing sound in the distance…

It's Simple, My Boy!

The Lord and Lady Dusbury of Challington Manor that my grandfather knew eventually died and were succeeded by the next generation. The new lord was determined that the old family seat should not be demolished, become a country club, a school or a hotel, and so he lead the way developing the estate business to ensure that prosperity continued. He also married Monique, a delightful French girl, about twenty years younger than him. She quickly became part of the community and charmed everybody with her winning smile and genuinely friendly manner. Even though her English was excellent some of the older Whytteford residents had a little difficulty understanding her accent but really she spoke the language more grammatically than they did. Somehow Monique usually managed to comprehend the rustic tongue of The Forest but if she was in doubt she would gently say, 'Zat is zo interesting.' She would then nod and give a dazzling smile that overcame any doubts that a villager might have.

Monique was a lady who knew many people from the world of the arts and one year she invited distinguished musicians to visit the manor and give the first Challington Festival. The format was simple. As the great hall of the manor could comfortably seat over one hundred guests a dais was erected and the musicians performed with portraits of past generations of the Dusbury family staring down at them seeming to either approve or grimace at the performers. There was a piano recital, a string quartet performed and one evening was devoted to the music of Mozart. String players were joined by a pianist and woodwind soloists for performances of some of the great composer's finest chamber works.

Monique had persuaded many local people to give their support. Ella Landy was coaxed out of retirement and talked into creating spectacular flower arrangements. At first she grumbled and muttered, 'I thought I had finished with this place.' Secretly she was thrilled to have been asked and when the displays were complete her muttering changed to, 'Quite like the old times! If only dear old Lady D could see this! Just like the old times.'

'You will come and help with our feztival, won't you?' was Monique's persuasive line and few refused.

Old Harry just said, 'Ah, Aaaah!' and as Monique couldn't translate this she took it for a refusal when in fact he thought he had agreed to help. Harry turned up before the concerts and was put on parking duty.

'Come and help at ze Mozart night,' Monique said to me. 'You'll love it. Ztay for ze party afterwards as well,' she added, 'then you'll meet ze players.'

It was a lovely midsummer evening and The Forest had an air of tranquillity that was soothing and relaxing. I walked to the manor and enjoyed the warmth of the evening sun. The guests arrived with picnic hampers ready for the interval and settled down for an evening of pleasure. The windows of the great hall were left open and Mozart's magical music wafted over the grounds and into the trees. First a flute quartet full of jollity, was played and then Bertram Major, a very distinguished player, performed the oboe quartet. It was sublime and fitted the setting and the balmy evening to perfection. He played with astonishing ease and like most oboe players could mould long phrases seemingly without breathing.

When it was time for an interval, which lasted an hour, the audience spread themselves and their picnics over the lawns, bottles were opened, champagne corks popped and the air was full of the scents of summer flowers, rich paté, smoked salmon and alcohol.

'Come on, Bertie,' Monique said to the oboist. 'Come and have zome champagne. You've earned it.' And she picked up a glass and passed it to him.

'Ah! You know my weaknesses!' declared Bertie. 'Cheers!' He quaffed the glass of champagne in one draft. I stared in amazement.

'Bertie always does zat,' said Monique.

'Need a quick drink after a performance,' explained Bertie as he took another glass. 'It scarcely affects me. Hardly know I've drunk it.'

'Take care of Bertie,' said Monique and she moved away to attend to other musicians.

I took a glass of champagne and had a sip.

'What did you think of it?' asked Bertie, who had now nearly finished his second glass.

'It's delicious.'

'Not the champagne, the music!' There was an old world and elegant charm about Bertie. His eyes twinkled and his little moustache emphasised his manner and his smile.

'Oh, sorry! I love Mozart and that's a gorgeous piece.'

'I'm pretty good at it, play it jolly well.' There was no false modesty about Bertie.

'Can I ask you something?'

'Anything, my boy, as long as it's not about my sex life!' The blue eyes twinkled again.

'How do you manage to play such long…?'

I didn't have a chance to finish my sentence as Monique called to him.

'Bertie come and meet…' and he wandered over to another part of the garden collecting his third glass of champagne on the way.

Eventually Monique walked round the garden ringing a little bell, as the interval was over, and the audience returned to the hall. I looked for Bertie who was chatting happily to a beautiful, tall, slender girl nearly thirty years younger than him. This was Huguette, Monique's younger sister, who was visiting because of the festival. She looked very attractive in pastel summer dress that clung to her bronzed body and emphasised every elegant curve.

'Let's stay outside,' Bertie said to her. He was clearly attracted by Huguette. 'We'll hear the music just as well and we can drink more champagne.'

Soon the delights of Mozart's music were drifting over the garden again and an air of enchantment spread everywhere. Bertie and Huguette sat close together on a garden bench and when the concert had finished there were two empty champagne bottles by the seat.

Champagne corks popped and the air was full of the scents of summer…

The strange thing was that all this alcohol seemed to have little effect on Bertie. He spoke clearly without an increase in volume, he was charming and courteous to everybody and having given his performance he was very much at ease. After the concert the audience drifted away and Monique rounded up her guests.

'Lots of food in ze dining room,' she declared, 'champagne too.'

'That's good,' said Bertie. 'I was feeling rather parched.' As they stood up Bertie wrapped an arm round Huguette and I noticed he swiftly zipped up the back of her dress.

Having enjoyed plenty of champagne and delicious food I thought that I should leave.

'Thank you for a lovely evening,' I said to Monique. 'It was wonderful.'

'You can't pozzibly leave zo early,' she replied. 'What's the 'urry?'

'I came on foot. I really need to go.'

'Nonzense, I'll make sure you get a lift home. Have zome more champagne.' And she calmly refilled my glass.

After another hour of champagne, humour and wellbeing the party was breaking up.

'Let's arrange a lift juzt for you,' said Monique. Her eyes searched the room. 'Ah, Bertie will take you. He's ztaying with friends and will be going your way.'

I was horrified. As Bertie had been drinking so freely I had assumed that he would be staying at the manor.

'Are you sure, after all he's…'

'He won't mind,' said Monique. 'He's very sociable. Look how he's chatting to my zister.' By now Huguette and Bertie were nearly horizontal on a sofa, she was wrapped round him with almost all of her long suntanned legs on display. Bertie's hands were softly appreciating Huguette and they were occasionally exchanging more than friendly kisses. 'I think it's time he went anyway,' added Monique.

After Huguette and Bertie had exchanged prolonged farewell kisses I climbed into Bertie's Jaguar. He placed his precious oboe in the boot then sat in the driving seat.

'Nice to have some company,' he said and we set off. His driving was perfect. He stopped smoothly in all the right places, used his indicators and the car purred softly along the roads of The Forest.

Suddenly he gently applied the brakes. 'What's all this?' he said. A policeman had flagged us down. Bertie stopped and wound down the car window. The policeman looked in.

'Good evening, officer,' said Bertie. 'Have I committed an offence?'

'Certainly not, sir,' said the policeman. 'We are just carrying out some random breathalyser tests. Have you had any alcohol this evening?'

'Well,' said Bertie, 'I did have a glass of champagne at the concert.'

'Then we must test you, sir. Could you get out of the car please?'

Aghast to hear these words I remained in my seat and stayed silent.

Bertie stood talking amicably to the policeman as if he hadn't a care in the world. The officer produced the breathalyser.

'Now blow into this, please, sir.'

'Very well; I've been longing to try one of these things.'

'Then perhaps this is your lucky night, sir.'

Bertie did as he was asked and returned the equipment.

'Now, we just wait a few seconds for the result.'

We waited and Bertie asked the officer a few friendly questions.

'Do you often do this in The Forest?'

'Not usually, but as there's the festival at Challington Manor we thought a few drivers might be over the limit.'

'How interesting,' said Bertie. 'Have you caught many?'

'Not yet, sir.' There was a hint of frustration and menace in the officer's voice. 'But I expect we will soon,' he added.

'You are doing very important work,' Bertie said affably.

'Now, let's look at the result,' said the policeman. He studied the breathalyser carefully. 'Right, all clear, sir.' He sounded very disappointed. 'I suppose you can go.' It was a good thing he didn't look into the Jaguar as he would have seen me sitting rigid with a look of astonishment on my face and with my mouth wide open.

'Thank you,' said Bertie. 'Keep up the good work!' He climbed in to the Jaguar, turned the ignition and the car gently moved away.

After we had travelled about a mile I could not contain my curiosity any longer.

'How did you do it?'

'Do what?' Bertie feigned innocence but really knew why I was asking this question.

'Pass the breathalyser test.'

'That's easy, my boy.' He laughed quietly and had a cheeky gleam in his eyes. 'I am an oboist and I'm a damned good one. Earlier this evening you were about to ask me a question. Ask it again.'

'How do you manage to play such long phrases without seeming to take a breath?'

'The answer is circular breathing. As an oboist I have to do it and the technique comes in very handy at other times. The breath never gets down into my lungs. It's in through the nose and out through the oboe.'

'That's really clever.'

'And just now the air went in my nose and out to the breathalyser. Never touched my lungs. It's simple, my boy! It's something you should learn. It might come in useful one day!'

He dropped me off near my home in Whytteford.

'Thank you for the lift,' I said. 'Do you know the way to where you are staying?'

'Actually I'm going back to the manor.' Bertie gave a twinkling smile.

'Have you forgotten something, then?'

'No. Certainly not!' He gave a gentle purr of delight. 'I must go now. I've arranged something with Huguette. I mustn't keep her waiting!'

Roses, Roses All The Way…

When World War Two broke out many of the young men of The Forest were called to join the forces and one of them was William who came from Chamford. He was not yet twenty years old. His parents were sad that he had to leave them but knew that he was doing the right thing. He was posted for training miles away in another part of the country where the rugged scenery contrasted with the sylvan woodlands of his home.

In a little town, near where Will had been posted, two young ladies wearing summer dresses were laughing and talking. Another one joined them, she liked the others but did not know them very well. They got on happily enough but they were not among her true friends.

'We're going to see a lady who tells fortunes.'

'Why don't you come with us, Marjorie? It's just a bit of fun.'

Marjorie hesitated. Did she really want to do this? She thought for a moment. 'Yes, I'll come,' she said.

'When shall we go?'

'Can we all go on Thursday?'

And on Thursday afternoon they set off. First there was a train ride; followed by a bus journey and then a long walk until eventually they came to a quiet village. It was early summer and the countryside was decked in fresh green leaves and the hedgerows were busy with birds. Down a short lane they found a tiny cottage. The girls knocked on the door and a short elderly lady with a serious look but alert eyes answered.

'Hello,' she said, 'why are you here?'

'We've come to have our fortunes told.'

'I'm sorry, my dears, I can't do that. My husband has told me I have to stop. He doesn't like me doing it. It makes me too tired.'

'But we've come a long way. Can't you help us?'

'We'll pay you.'

The old lady hesitated.

'Please be kind to us. We promise that we will never tell anyone where you live.'

'Very well, my husband is away today. I'll see you one at a time in my front room.'

After the first two girls had been seen each of them came out from the cottage smiling and laughing.

'It's your turn now, Marjorie.'

Marjorie went in to the little cottage.

'Come and sit down, my dear.' The little lady looked at her intently. 'Now hold this in your hands.' She placed a crystal ball in Marjorie's hands.

'What…what?' Marjorie gasped as she had felt a curious sensation pass through her.

'You felt something, then, didn't you?'

'Yes I did. It…it…it was like an electric shock.'

'Let me see now.'

The old lady studied the crystal ball for long moments, her gaze unmoving, and then she lifted her eyes.

The old lady studied the crystal ball for long moments.

'I can see you have had a lot of unhappiness in recent years but I can tell you that the unhappy times have now passed. You are going out with someone connected with the law. Keep away from him; he will not be good for you. Before a month has passed you will meet a man with fair hair, twinkling eyes and he will be singing. You will fall in love and before the year is out you will have married him. The future will have its ups and downs, but as I say, your unhappy times are over and from now on your life will be roses, roses all the way.'

Marjorie was amazed. How could the old lady know these things? True, two of her brothers had been killed during the war, that was sad, but how could the woman foretell her future? She was certainly wrong about one thing.

'But I don't know anyone connected with the law.'

'Yes, you do, think about it. You do know someone connected with the law and you must stay away from him. Think of a man in blue clothes, think about him.'

'I really don't know anyone to do with the law.'

'Yes you do,' said the lady. 'Think carefully.'

Marjorie and her companions left the cottage and began the journey home. Two of them chattered as they walked and continued on the return train, but Marjorie was almost silent. Suddenly she gasped.

'What is it?'

'Something that lady said.'

'What? What did she say?'

'Never mind, I must think about it.'

Marjorie had realised that the old lady had been right. She was going out with someone connected with the law. She often saw a member of staff who worked at a nearby borstal. Of course, that was the man connected with the law!

The soldiers that were stationed in the area would attend dances in nearby villages and they were popular with the young ladies. One July evening, not long after the fortune-telling episode, Marjorie went to one of the dances. Some soldiers arrived, smartly dressed in their uniforms. One of them had fair hair and sparkling eyes and he was singing a popular song.

'I've got sixpence: jolly, jolly sixpence
I've got sixpence to last me all my life.'

He saw Marjorie and his heart leapt at the sight of this petite dark-haired beauty. He thought that here was a girl with personality as well as good looks.

'Will you dance with me?'

This handsome man whisked Marjorie on to the floor and while they were dancing together he was singing and laughing.

'Who are you?' she asked and she felt happy and safe with this cheerful man.

'I'm Will. Who are you?'

'I'm Marjorie.'

'Let's dance.'

Will was a good dancer and he found dancing with Marjorie made him feel very content. In the slower dances he held her close to him and she didn't resist. The romance blossomed and she felt so happy when Will proposed to her.

Marjorie would have returned to the little cottage and told the fortune-teller that she had been right about everything but she had no idea where to go.

Their marriage took place before the end of the year in a time of shortages and so Will and Marjorie had no wedding cake, but they didn't mind. At Christmas William proudly took his new wife home and showed her The Forest and as it was winter the gorse was in full bloom.

Their marriage lasted over sixty years and although they encountered the ups and downs of life for them it was, 'Roses, roses all the way.'